Venus Unbound

Venus Unbound

Anonymous

CARROLL & GRAF PUBLISHERS, INC.
New York

Copyright © 1985 by Carroll & Graf Publishers, Inc.

All rights reserved. No part of this book may be reproduced or utilized in any form or by any means without permission from the publisher.

First Carroll & Graf edition 1985
Second printing 1988

Original titles: FLOSSIE: A VENUS AT FIFTEEN and EVELINE

Carroll & Graf Publishers, Inc.
260 Fifth Avenue
New York, NY 10001

ISBN: 0-88184-159-5

Manufactured in the United States of America

FLOSSIE

PREFACE

IN PRESENTING TO A CRITICAL PUBLIC THIS narrative of a delightful experience, I am conscious of an inability to do justice to the indescribable charm of my subject.

A true daughter of the Paphian goddess, Flossie added to the erotic allurements inherited from her immortal mother a sense of humour which is not traceable in any of the proceedings on Mount Ida or elsewhere. Those of my readers, who have had the rare good fortune to meet with the combination, will not gainsay my assertion that it is an incomparable incentive to deeds of love.

If some of those deeds, as here set down, should seem to appertain to a somewhat advanced school of amatory action, I beg objectors

Flossie: a Venus of fifteen

to remember that Flossie belongs to the end of
the century, *when such things are done*, to the
safety, comfort and delight of vast numbers of
fair English girls, and to the unspeakable enjoyment of their adorers.

* *Credo experto.* *

So, in the words of the City toastmaster: —
"Pray silence, gentlemen, for your heroine,
Flossie: a Venus of Fifteen."

J. A.

POSTSCRIPT. — Flossie has herself revised
this unpretending work, and has added a foot-
note here and there which she trusts may not
be regarded as painful interruptions to a truthful
tale.

All thine the new wine of desire
  The fruit of four lips as they clung
Till the hair and the eyelids took fire;
  The fan of a serpentine tongue,
The froth of the serpents of pleasure,
  More salt than the foam of the sea,
Now felt as a flame, now at leisure
        As wine-shed for me!

They were purple of rainment, and golden,
  Filled full of thee, fiery with wine,
Thy lovers, in haunts unbeholden,
  In marvellous chambers of thine.
They are fled and their footprints escape us
  Who appraise thee, adore, and abstain,
O daughter of Death and Priamus!
        Our Lady of Pain.
                    A. C. Swinburne

CHAPTER I

"My love, she's but a lassie yet"

TOWARDS THE END OF A BRIGHT SUNNY AFTER-
noon in June, I was walking in one of the quieter
streets of Piccadilly, when my eye was caught
by two figures coming in my direction. One
was that of a tall, finely-made woman about
27, who would under other circumstances, have
received something more than an approving
glance. But it was her companion that rivetted
my gaze of almost breathless admiration. This
was a young girl of fifteen, of such astounding
beauty of face and figure as I had never seen
or dreamt of. Masses of bright, wavy, brown
hair fell to her waist. Deep violet eyes looked
out from under long curling lashes, and seemed
to laugh in unison with the humorous curves of
the full red lips. These and a thosand other
charms I was to know by heart later on, but
what struck me most at this view, was the extraordinary size and beauty of the girl's bust,
shown to all possible advantage by her dress

15

Flossie: a Venus of fifteen

which, in the true artistic French style, crept in between her breasts, outlining their full and perfect form with loving fidelity. Tall and lithe, she moved like a young goddess, her short skirt shewing the action of a pair of exquisitely moulded legs, to which the tan-coloured open-work silk stockings were plainly designed to invite attention. Unable to take my eyes from this enchanting vision, I was approaching the pair, when to my astonishment, the elder lady suddenly spoke my name.

"You do not remember me, Captain Archer." For a moment I was at a loss, but the voice gave me the clue.

"But I do," I answered, "you are Miss Letchford, who used to teach my sisters."

"Quite right. But I have given up teaching, for which fortunately there is no longer any necessity. I am living in a flat with my dear little friend here. Let me introduce you, — Flossie Eversley — Captain Archer."

The violet eyes laughed up at me; and the red lips parted in a merry smile. A dimple appeared at the corner of the mouth. I was done for! Yes; at thirty-five years of age, with more than my share of experiences in every phase of love, I went down before this lovely girl with her childish face smiling at me above

16

"My love, she's but a lassie yet"

the budding womanhood of her rounded breasts, and confessed myself defeated!

A moment of two later, I had passed from them with the address of the flat in my pocket, and under promise to go down to tea on the next day.

At midday I received the following letter:

Dear Captain Archer,

"I am sorry to be obliged to be out when you come; and yet not altogether sorry, because I should like you to know Flossie very well. She is an orphan, without a relation in the world. She is just back from a Paris school. In years she is of course a child, but in tact and knowledge she is a woman; also in figure, as you can see for yourself! She is of an exceedingly warm and passionate nature, and a look that you gave her yesterday was not lost upon her. In fact, to be quite frank, she has fallen in love with you! You will find her a delightful companion. Use her *very* tenderly, and she will do anything in the world for you. Speak to her about life in the French school; she loves to talk of it. I want her to be happy, and I think you can help. Remember she is only just fifteen.

"Yours sincerely,

"*Eva Letchford.*"

Flossie: a Venus of fifteen

I must decline any attempt to describe my feelings on receiving this remarkable communication. My first impulse was to give up the promised call at the flat. But the flower-like face, the soft red lips and the laughing eyes passed before my mind's eye, followed by an instant vision of the marvelous breasts and the delicate shapely legs in their brown silk stockings, and I knew that fate was too strong for me. For it was of course impossible to misunderstand the meaning of Eva Letchford's letter, and indeed, when I reached the flat, she herself opened the door to me, whispering as she passed out, "Flossie is in there, waiting for you. You two can have the place to yourselves. One last word. You have been much in Paris, have you not? So has Flossie. She is *very* young — *and there are ways* — Good-bye."

I passed into the next room. Flossie was curled up in a long chair, reading. Twisting her legs from under her petticoats with a sudden movement that brought into full view her delicately embroidered drawers, she rose and came towards me, a rosy flush upon her cheeks, her eyes shining, her whole bearing instinct with an enchanting mixture of girlish coyness and anticipated pleasure. Her short white skirt swayed as she moved across the room, her

18

"My love, she's but a lassie yet"

breasts stood out firm and round under the close-fitting woven silk jersey; what man of mortal flesh and blood could withstand such allurements as these! Not I, for one! In a moment, she was folded in my arms. I rained kisses on her hair, her forehead, her eyes, her cheeks, and then, grasping her body closer and always closer to me, I glued my lips upon the scarlet mouth and revelled in a long and maddeningly delicious kiss — a kiss to be ever remembered — so well remembered now, indeed, that I must make some attempt to describe it. My hands were behind Flossie's head, buried in her long brown hair. Her arms were round my body, locked and clinging. At the first impact, her lips were closed, but a moment later they parted, and slowly, gently, almost as if in the performance of some solemn duty, the rosy tongue crept into my mouth, and bringing with it a flood of the scented juices from her throat, curled amorously round my own, whilst her hands dropped to my buttocks, and standing on tiptoe, she drew me to her with such extraordinary to be already in conjunction. Not a word was spoken on either side — indeed, under the circumstances, speech was impossible, for our tongues had twined together in a caress of unspeakable sweetness, which neither would be the

Flossie: a Venus of fifteen

first to forego. At last, the blood was coursing through my veins at a pace that became unbearable and I was compelled to unglue my mouth from hers. Still silent, but with love and longing in her eyes, she pressed me into a low chair, and seating herself on the arm, passed her hand behind my head, and looking full into my eyes, whispered my name in accents that were like the sound of a running stream. I kissed her open mouth again and again, and then, feeling that the time had come for some little explanation:

"How long will it be before your friend Eva comes back?" I asked.

"She has gone down into the country, and won't be here till late this evening."

"Then I may stay with you, may I?"

"Yes, do, do, *do*, Jack. Do you know, I have got seats for an Ibsen play to-night, I was wondering . . . if . . . you would . . . take me!"

"Take *you* — to an Ibsen play — with your short frocks, and all that hair down your back! Why, I don't believe they'd let us in?"

"Oh, if *that's* all, wait a minute."

She skipped out of the room with a whisk of her petticoats and a free display of brown silk legs. Almost before I had time to wonder what she was up to, she was back again. She had put on a long skirt of Eva's, her hair was coiled on

"My love, she's but a lassie yet"

the top of her head, she wore my "billycock" hat and a pair of blue pincenez, and carrying a crutch-handled stick, she advanced upon me with a defiant air, and glaring down over the top of her glasses, she said in a deep masculine voice:

"Now, sir if you're ready for Ibsen, *I* am. Or if your tastes are so *low* that you can't care about a play, I'll give you a skirtdance."

As she said this, she tore off the long dress, threw my hat on to a sofa, let down her hair with a turn of the wrist, and motioning me to the piano, picked up her skirts and began to dance.

Enchanted as I was by the humour of her quick change to the "Ibsen woman," words are vain to describe my feelings as I feebly tinkled a few bars on the piano and watched the dancer.

Every motion was the perfection of grace and yet no Indian Nautch-girl could have more skillfully expressed the idea of sexual allurement. Gazing at her in speechless admiration, I saw the violet eyes glow with passion, the full red lips part, the filmy petticoats were lifted higher and higher; the loose frilled drawers gleamed white. At last breathless and panting, she fell back upon a chair, her eyes closed, her legs parted, her breasts heaving. A mingled perfume came to my nostrils — half *"odor di faemina,"*

21

Flossie: a Venus of fifteen

half the scent of white rose from her hair and clothes.

I flung myself upon her.

"Tell me, Flossie darling, what shall I do first?

The answer came, quick and short.

"Kiss me — *between my legs!*"

In an instant, I was kneeling before her. Her legs fell widely apart. Sinking to a sitting posture, I plunged my head between her thighs. The petticoats incommoded me a little, but I soon managed to arrive at the desired spot. Somewhat to my surprise, instead of finding the lips closed and barricaded as is usual in the case of young girls, they were ripe, red and pouting, and as my mouth closed eagerly upon the delicious orifice and my tongue found and pressed upon the trembling clitoris, I knew that my qualms of conscience had been vain. My utmost powers were now called into play and I sought, by every means I possessed, to let Flossie know that I was no halfbaked lover. Passing my arms behind her, I extended my tongue to its utmost length and with rapid agile movements penetrated the scented recesses. Her hands locked themselves under my head, soft gasps of pleasure came for her lips, and as I delivered at last an effective attack upon the

"My love, she's but a lassie yet"

erect clitoris, her fingers clutched my neck, and with a sob of delight, she crossed her legs over my back, and pressing my head towards her, held me with a convulsive grasp, whilst the aromatic essence of her being flowed softly into my enchanted mouth.

As I rose to my feet, she covered her face with her hands and I saw a blue eye twinkle out between the fingers with an indescribable mixture of bashfulness and fun. Then, as if suddenly remembering her self, she sat up, dropped her petticoats over her knees, and looking up at me from under the curling lashes, said in a tone of profound melancholy.

"Jack, am I not a *disgraceful* child! All the same, I wouldn't have missed *that* for a million pounds."

"Nor would I, little sweetheart; and whenever you would like to have it again —"

"No, no, it is your turn now."

"What! Flossie; you don't mean to say —"

"But I *do* mean to say it, and to *do* it too. Lie down on that sofa at once, sir."

"But, Flossie, I really — "

Without another word she leapt at me, threw her arms round my neck and fairly bore me down on to the divan. Falling on the top of me, she twined her silken legs round mine and gently

Flossie: a Venus of fifteen

pushing the whole of her tongue between my lips, began to work her body up and down with a wonderful sinuous motion which soon brought me to a state of excitement bordering on frenzy. Then, shaking a warning finger at me to keep still, she slowly slipped to her knees on the floor.

In another moment, I felt the delicate fingers round my straining yard. Carrying it to her mouth she touched it ever so softly with her tongue; then slowly parting her lips she pushed it gradually between them, keeping a grasp of the lower end with her hand which she moved gently up and down. Soon the tongue began to quicken its motion, and the brown head to work rapidly in a perpendicular direction. I buried my hands under the lovely hair, and clutched the white neck towards me, plunging the nut further and further into the delicious mouth until I seemed almost to touch the uvula. Her lips, tongue and hands now worked with redoubled ardour, and my sensations became momentarily more acute, until with a cry I besought her to let me withdraw. Shaking her head with great emphasis, she held my yard in a firmer grasp, and passing her disengaged hand behind me, drew me towards her face, and with an unspeakable clinging action of her mouth, carried

24

"My love, she's but a lassie yet"

out the delightful act of love to its logical conclusion, declining to remove her lips until, some minutes after, the last remaining evidences of the late crisis had completely disappeared.

Then and not till then, she stood up, and bending over me, as I lay, kissed me on the forehead, whispering: —

"There! Jack, now I love you twenty times more than ever." *)

I gazed into the lovely face in speechless adoration.

"Why don't you say something?" she cried. "Is there anything else you want me to do?"

"Yes," I answered, "there is."

"Out with it, then."

"I am simply dying to see your breasts, naked."

"Why, you darling, of course, you shall! Stay there a minute."

Off she whisked again, and almost before I could realise she had gone, I looked up and she was before me. She had taken off everything but her chemise and stockings, the former lowered beneath her breasts.

---

*) "This is a fact, as every girl knows who has ever gamahuched and been gamahuched by the man or boy she loves. As a *link*, it beats fucking out of the field. I've tried both and I *know*." *Flossie*

25

Flossie: a Venus of fifteen

Any attempt to describe the beauties thus laid bare to my adoring gaze must necessarily fall absurdly short of the reality. Her neck, throat and arms were full and exquisitely rounded, bearing no trace of juvenile immaturity.

Her breasts, however, were of course the objects of my special and immediate attention.

For size, perfection of form and colour, I had never seen their equals, nor could the mind of man conceive anything so alluring as the coral nipples which stood out firm and erect, craving kisses. A wide space intervened between the two snowy hillocks which heaved a little with the haste of her late exertions, I gazed a moment in breathless delight and admiration, then rushing towards her, I buried my face in the enchanting valley, passed my burning lips over each of the neighbouring slopes and finally seized upon one after the other of the rosy nipples, which I sucked, mouthed and tongued with a frenzy or delight.

The darling little girl lent herself eagerly to my every action, pushing her nipples into my mouth and eyes, pressing her breasts against my face, and clinging to my neck with her lovely naked arms.

Whilst we were thus amorously employed, my little lady had contrived dexterously to slip

26

"My love, she's but a lassie yet"

out of her chemise, and now stood before me naked but for her brown silk stockings and little shoes.

"There, Mr. Jack, now you can see my breasts, and everything else that you like of mine. In future, this will be my full-dress costume for making love to you in. Stop, though; it wants just one touch." And darting out of the room, she came back with a beautiful chain of pearls round her neck, finishing with a pendant of rubies which hung just low enough to nestle in the Valley of Delight, between the wonderful breasts.

"I am, now," she said, "The White Queen of the Gama Huchi Islands. My kingdom is bounded on this side by the piano, and on the other by the furthest edge of the bed in the next room. Any male person found wearing a *stitch* of clothing within those boundaries will be sentenced to lose his p . . . . but soft! who comes here?"

Shading her eyes with her hand she gazed in my direction: —

"Aha! a stranger; and, unless these royal eyes deceive us, a man! He shall see what it is to defy our laws! What ho! within there! Take this person and remove his p . . . ."

"Great Queen!" I said, in a voice of deep

27

Flossie: a Venus of fifteen

humility, "if you will but grant me two minutes, I will make haste to comply with your laws."

"And we, good fellow, will help you. *(Aside.)*

"Methinks he is somewhat comely*). *(Aloud.)*

"But first let us away with these garments, which are more than aught else a violation of our Gama Huchian Rules, Good! now the shirt. And what, pray, it *this?* We thank you, sir, but we are not requiring any *tent-poles* just now."

"Then if your Majesty will deign to remove your royal fingers I will do my humble best to cause the offending pole to disappear. At present, with your Majesty's hand upon it — !"

"Silence, Sir! Your time is nearly up, and if the last garment be not removed in twenty seconds . . . So! you obey. Tis well! You shall see how we reward a faithful subject of our laws." And thrusting my yard between her lips, the Great White Queen of the Gama Huchi Islands sucked in the whole column to the very root, and by dint of working her royal mouth up and down, and applying her royal fingers to the neighbour-

---

*) Don't believe I ever said anything of the sort, but if I did, "methinks" I'd better take this opportunity of withdrawing the statement. *Flossie*

"My love, she's but a lassie yet"

ing appendages, soon drew into her throat a tribute to her greatness, which, from its volume and the time it took in the act of payment, plainly caused her Majesty the most exquisite enjoyment. Of my own pleasure I will only say that it was delirious, whilst in this, as in all other love sports in which we indulged, an added zest was given by the humour and fancy with which this adorable child-woman designed and carried out our amusements. In the present case, the personating of the Great White Queen appeared to afford her especial delight, and going on with the performance, she took a long branch of pampasgrass from its place and waving it over my head, she said: —

"The next ceremony to be performed by a visitor to these realms will, we fear, prove somewhat irksome, but it must be gone through. We shall now place our royal person on this lofty throne. You, sir, will sit upon this footstool before us. We shall then wave our sceptre three times. At the third wave, our knees will part and our guest will see before him the royal spot of love. This he will proceed to salute with a kiss which shall last until we are pleased to signify that we have had enough. Now, most noble guest, open your mouth, *don't* shut your eyes, and prepare! One, two, *three*."

29

Flossie: a Venus of fifteen

The pampas-grass waved, the legs parted, and nestling between the ivory thighs, I saw the scarlet lips open and show the erected clitoris peeping forth from its nest below the slight brown tuft which adorned the base of the adorable belly. I gazed and gazed in mute rapture, until a sharp strident voice above me said: —

"Now then, there, move on, please; can't have you blocking up the road all day!" Then changing suddenly to her own voice: —

"Jack, if you don't kiss me at once I shall *die!*"

I pressed towards the delicious spot and taking the whole cunt into my mouth passed my tongue upwards along the perfumed lips until it met the clitoris, which thrust itself amourously between my lips, imploring kisses. These I rained upon her with all the ardour I could command, clutching the rounded bottom with feverish fingers and drawing the naked belly closer and ever closer to my burning face, whilst my tongue plunged deep within the scented cunt and revelled in its divine odours and the contraction of its beloved lips.

The Great White Queen seemed to relish this particular form of homage, for it was many minutes before the satin thighs closed, and with the little hands under my chin, she raised my

30

"My love, she's but a lassie yet"

face and looking into my eyes with inexpressible love and sweetness shining from her own, she said simply: —

"Thank you, Jack. You're a darling!" —

By way of answer I covered her with kisses, omitting no single portion of the lovely naked body, the various beauties of which lent themselves with charming zest to my amorous doings. Upon the round and swelling breasts, I lavished renewed devotion, sucking the rosy nipples with a fury of delight, and relishing to the full the quick movements of rapture with which the lithe clinging form was constantly shaken, no less than the divine aroma passing to my nostrils as the soft thighs opened and met again, the rounded arms rose and fell, and with this, the faintly perfumed hair brushing my face and shoulders mingled its odour of tea-rose.

All this was fast exciting my senses to the point of madness, and there were moments when I felt that to postpone much longer the consummation of our amour would be impossible.

I looked at the throbbing breasts, remembered the fragrant lips below that had pouted ripely to meet my kisses, the developed clitoris that told of joys long indulged in. And then . . . And then . . . the sweet girlish face looked up into mine, the violet eyes seemed to take on a plead-

31

Flossie: a Venus of fifteen

ing expression, and as if reading my thoughts, Flossie pushed me gently into a chair, seated herself on my knee, slipped an arm round my neck, and pressing her cheek to mine, whispered: —

"Poor, *poor* old thing! I know what it wants; and *I* want it too — badly, oh! so badly. But, Jack, you can't guess what a friend Eva has been to me, and I've promised her *not to!* You see I'm only just fifteen, and . . . *the consequences!* There! don't let us talk about it. Tell me all about yourself, and then I'll tell you about me. When you're tired of hearing me talk, you shall stop my mouth with — well, whatever you like. Now sir, begin!"

I gave her a short narrative of my career from boyhood upwards, dry and dull enough in all conscience!

"Yes, yes, that's all very nice and prim and proper," she cried. "But you haven't told me the principal thing of all — when you first began to be — naughty, and with whom?"

I invented some harmless fiction which, I saw, the quickwitted little girl did not believe, and begged her to tell me her own story, which she at once proceeded to do. I shall endeavour to transcribe it, though it is impossible to convey any idea of the humour with which it was

32

"My love, she's but a lassie yet"

delivered, still less of the irrepressible fun which flashed from her eyes at the recollection of her schoolgirl pranks and amourettes. There were, of course, many interruptions*), for most of which I was probably responsible; but, on the whole, in the following chapter will be found a fairly faithful transcript of Flossie's early experiences. Some at least of these I am sanguine, will be thought to have been of a sufficiently appetising character.

---

*) The first of these is a really serious one, but for this the impartial reader will see that the responsibility was divided.

CHAPTER II

"How Flossie Acquired the French tongue."

BEFORE I BEGIN, JACK, I SHOULD LIKE TO hold something nice and solid in my hand, to sort of give me confidence as I go on. Have you got anything about you that would do?"

I presented what seemed to me the most suitable article 'in stock' at the moment.

"Aha!" said Flossie in an affected voice, "the very thing! How *very* fortunate that you should happen to have it ready!"

"Well, madam, you see it is an article we are constantly being asked for by our lady-customers. It is rather an expensive thing — seven pound ten —"

"Yes, it's rather stiff. Still, if you can assure me that it will always keep in its present condition, I shouldn't mind spending a good deal upon it."

"You will find, madam, that anything you may spend upon it will be amply returned to

35

Flossie: a Venus of fifteen

you. Our ladies have always expressed the greatest satisfaction with it."

"Do you mean that you find they come more than once? If so, I'll take it now."

"Perhaps you would allow me to bring it myself —?"

"Thanks, but I think I can hold it quite well in my hand. It won't go off suddenly, will it?"

"Not if it is kept in a cool place, madam."

"And it mustn't be shaken, I suppose, like *that*, for instance?" (shaking it.)

"For goodness gracious sake, take your hand away, Flossie, or there'll be a catastrophe."

"That is a good word, Jack! But do you suppose that if I saw a 'catastrophe' coming I shouldn't know what to do with it?"

"*What* should you do?"

"Why, what *can* you do with a catastrophe of that sort but *swallow it?*"

The effect of this little interlude upon us both was magnetic. Instead of going on with her story, Flossie commanded me to lie upon my back on the divan, and having placed a couple of pillows under my neck, knelt astride of me with her face towards my feet. With one or two caressing movements of her bottom, she arranged herself so that the scarlet vulva rested

36

"How Flossie acquired the French tongue"

just above my face. Then gently sinking down, she brought her delicious cunt full upon my mouth from which my tongue instantly darted to penetrate the adorable recess. At the same moment, I felt the brown hair fall upon my thighs, my straining prick plunged between her lips, and was engulphed in her velvet mouth to the very root, whilst her hands played with feverish energy amongst the surrounding parts, and the nipples of her breasts rubbed softly against my belly.

In a very few moments, I had received into my mouth her first tribute of love and was working with might and main to procure a second, whilst she in her turn, wild with pleasure my wandering tongue was causing her, grasped my yard tightly between her lips, passing them rapidly up and down its whole length, curling her tongue round the nut, and maintaining all the time an ineffable sucking action which very soon produced its natural result. As I poured a torrent into her eager mouth, I felt the soft lips which I was kissing contract for a moment upon my tongue and then part again to set free the aromatic flood to which the intensity of her sensations imparted additional volume and sweetness.

The pleasure, we were both experiencing from

37

Flossie: a Venus of fifteen

this the most entrancing of all the reciprocal acts of love, was too keen to be abandoned after one effort. Stretching my hands upwards to mould and press the swelling breasts and erected nipples, I seized the rosy clitoris anew between my lips, whilst Flossie resumed her charming operations upon my instrument which she gamahuched with ever increasing zest and delight, and even with a skill and variety of action which would have been marvellous in a woman of double her age and experience. Once again the fragrant dew was distilled upon my enchanted tongue, and once again the velvet mouth closed upon my yard to receive the results of its divinely pleasurable ministrations.

Raising herself slowly and almost reluctantly from her position, Flossie laid her naked body at full length upon mine, and after many kisses upon my mouth, eyes and cheeks said, "Now you may go and refresh yourself with a bath while I dress for dinner."

"But where are we going to dine?" I asked.

"You'll see presently. *Go* along, there's a good boy!"

I did as I was ordered and soon came back from the bath-room, much refreshed by my welcome ablutions.

Five minutes later Flossie joined me, looking

38

"How Flossie acquired the French tongue"

lovelier than ever, in a short-sleeved pale blue muslin frock, cut excessively low in front, black openwork silk stockings and little embroidered shoes.

"Dinner is on the table," she said, taking my arm and leading me into an adjoining room where an exquisite little cold meal was laid out, to which full justice was speedily done, followed by coffee made by my hostess, who produced some Benedictine and a box of excellent cigars.

"There, Jack, if you're quite comfy, I'll go on with my story. Shall I stay here, or come and sit on your knee?"

"Well, as far as getting on with the story goes, I think you are better in that chair, Flossie —"

"But I told you I must have something to hold."

"You, you did, and the result was that we didn't get very far with the story, if you remember —"

"Remember! As if I was likely to forget. But look at this," holding up a rounded arm bare to the shoulder. "Am I to understand that you'd rather not have this round your neck?"

Needless to say she was to understand nothing of the sort, and a moment later she was perched upon my knee and having with deft penetrating

39

Flossie: a Venus of fifteen

fingers enough under her magic touch, began her narrative.

"I don't think there will be much to tell you until my school life at Paris begins. My father and mother both died when I was quite small; I had no brothers or sisters, and I don't believe I've got a relation in the world. You mustn't think I want to swagger, Jack, but I am rather rich. One of my two guardians died three years ago and the other is in India and doesn't care a scrap about me. Now and then, he writes and asks how I am getting on, and when he heard I was going to live with Eva (whom he knows quite well) he seemed perfectly satisfied. Two years ago he arranged for me to go to school in Paris.

"Now I must take great care not to shock you, but there's nothing for it but to tell you that about this time I began to have the most wonderful feelings all over me — a sort of desperate longing for something, — I didn't know what — which used to become almost unbearable when I danced or played any game in which a boy or man was near me. At the Paris school was a very pretty girl, named Ylette de Vespertin, who, for some reason I never could understand, took a fancy to me. She was two years older than I, had several brothers and boy cous-

40

"How Flossie acquired the French tongue"

ins at home, and being up to every sort of lark and mischief, was just the girl I wanted as confidante. Of course she had no difficulty in explaining the whole thing to me, and in the course of a day or two, I knew everything there was to know. On the third day of our talks Ylette slipped a note into my hand as I was going up to bed. Now, Jack, you must really go and look out of the window while I tell you what it said:

" '(Chérie,
"Si tu veux te faire sucer la langue, les seins et le con, viens dans mon lit toute nue ce soir. C'est moi qui te ferai voir les anges.
" 'Viens de suite à ton
" 'Ylette.' "

"I have rather a good memory, and even if I hadn't, I don't think I could ever forget the words of that note, for it was the beginning of a most delicious time for me.

"I suppose if I had been a well-regulated young person, I should have taken no notice of the invitation. As it was, I stripped myself naked in a brace of shakes, and flew to Ylette's bedroom which was next door to the one I occupied. I had not realized before what a beautifully made girl she was. Her last garment was

41

Flossie: a Venus of fifteen

just slipping from her as I came in, and I stared in blank admiration at her naked figure which was like a statue in the perfection of its lines. A furious longing to touch it seized me, and springing upon her, I passed my hands feverishly up and down her naked body, until grasping me round the waist, she half dragged, half carried me to the bed, laid me on the edge of it, and kneeling upon the soft rug, plunged her head between my legs, and bringing her lips to bear full upon the *other* lips before her, parted them with a peculiar action of the mouth and inserted her tongue with a sudden stroke which sent perfect waves of delight through my whole body, followed by still greater ecstasy when she went for the particular spot *you* know of, Jack — the one near the top, I mean — and twisting her tongue over it, under it, round it and across it, soon brought about the result she wanted, and in her own expressive phrase 'me faisait voir les anges'.

"Of course I had no experience, but I did my best to repay her for the pleasures he had given me, and as I happen to possess an extremely long and pointed tongue, and Ylette's cunt — oh Jack, *I've said it at last!* Go and look out of the window again; or better still, come and stop my naughty mouth with — I *meant* your tongue, but this will do better still. The wicked monster,

"How Flossie acquired the French tongue"

what a size he is! Now put both your hands behind my head, and push him in till he touches my throat. Imagine he is *somewhere else*, work like a demon, and for your life, don't stop until the very end of all things Ah! the dear, darling, delicious thing! How he throbs with excitement! I believe he can *see* my mouth waiting for him. Come, Jack, my darling, my beloved, let me gamahuche you. I want to feel this heavenly prick of yours between my lips and against my tongue, so that I may suck it and drain every drop that comes from it into my mouth. Now, Jack *now* . . ."

The red lips closed hungrily upon the object of their desire, the rosy tongue stretched itself amorously along the palpitating yard, and twice, the tide of love poured freely forth to be received with every sign of delight into the velvet mouth.

Nothing in my experience had ever approached the pleasure which I derived from the intoxicating contact of this young girl's lips and tongue upon my most sensitive parts, enhanced as it was by my love for her, which grew apace, and by her own intense delight in the adorable pastime. So keen indeed were the sensations she procured me that I was almost able to forget the deprivation laid upon me by Flossie's

43

Flossie: a Venus of fifteen

promise to her friend. Indeed, when I reflected upon her youth, and the unmatched beauty of her girlish shape with its slender waist, smooth satin belly and firm rounded breasts, the whole seemed too perfect a work of nature to be married — at least as yet — by the probable consequences of an act of coition carried to its logical conclusion by a pair of ardent lovers.

So I bent my head once more to its resting place between the snowy thighs, and again drew from my darling little mistress the fragrant treasures of love's sacred store house, lavished upon my clinging lips with gasps and sighs and all possible tokens of enjoyment in the giving.

After this it was time to part, and at Flossie's suggestion I undressed her, brushed out her silky hair and put her into bed. Lying on her white pillow, she looked so fair and like a child that I was for saying goodnight with just a single kiss upon her cheek. But this was not in accordance with her views on the subject. She sat up in bed, flung her arms round my neck, nestled her face against mine and whispered in my ear:

"I'll never give a promise again as long as I live."

It was an awful moment and my resolution all but went down under the strain. But I just managed to resist, and after one prolonged em-

44

"How Flossie acquired the French tongue"

brace, during which Flossie's tongue went twining and twisting round my own with an indescribably lascivious motion, I planted a farewell kiss full upon the nipple of her left breast, sucked it for an instant and fled from the room.

On reaching my own quarters I lit a cigar and sat down to think over the extraordinary good fortune by which I had chanced upon this unique liaison. It was plain to me that in Flossie I had encountered probably the only specimen of her class. A girl of fifteen, with all the fresh charm of that beautiful age united to the fascinnation of a passionate and amorous woman. Add to these a finely-strung temperament, a keen sense of humour, and the true artist's striving after thoroughness in all she did, and it will be admitted that all these qualities meeting in a person of quite faultless beauty were enough to justify the self-congratulations with which I contemplated my present luck, and the rosy visions of pleasure to come which hung about my waking and sleeping senses till the morning.

About midday I called at the flat. The door was opened to me by Eva Letchford.

"I am so glad to see you," she said. "Flossie is out on her bicycle, and I can say what I want to."

As she moved to the window to draw up the blind a little, I had a better opportunity of notic-

45

Flossie: a Venus of fifteen

ing into what a really splendid woman she had developed. Observing my glances of frank admiration, she sat down in a low easy chair opposite to me, crossed her shapely legs, and looking over at me with a bright pleasant smile, said:

"Now, Jack — I may call you Jack, of course, because we are all three going to be great friends — you had my letter the other day. No doubt you thought it a strange document, but when we know one another better, you will easily understand how I came to write it."

"My dear girl, I understand it already. You forget I have had several hours with Flossie. It was her happiness you wanted to secure, and I hope she will tell you our plan was successful"

"Flossie and I have no secrets. She has told me everything that passed between you. She has also told me what did *not* pass between you, and how you did not even try to make her break her promise to me."

"I should have been a brute if I had —"

"Then I am afraid nineteen men out of twenty are brutes — but that's neither here nor there. What I want you to know is that I appreciate your nice feeling, and that some day soon I shall with Flossie's consent take an opportunity of shewing that appreciation in a practical way."

46

"How Flossie acquired the French tongue"

Here she crossed her right foot high over the left knee and very leisurely removed an imaginary speck of dust from the shotsilk stocking.

"Now I must go and change my dress. You'll stay and lunch with us in the coffeeroom, won't you? — that's right. This is my bedroom. I'll leave the door open so that we can talk till Flossie comes. She promised to be in by one o'clock."

We chatted away on indifferent subjects whilst I watched with much satisfaction the operations of the toilette in the next room.

Presently a little cry of dismay reached me:

"Oh dear, oh dear! do come here a minute, Jack. I have pinched one of my breasts with my stays and made a little red mark. Look! *Do* you think it will shew in evening dress?"

I examined the injury with all possible care and deliberation.

"My professional opinion is, madam, that as the mark is only an inch above the nipple we may fairly hope —"

"*Above* the nipple! then I'm afraid it will be a near thing," said Eva with a merry laugh.

"Perhaps a little judicious stroking by an experienced hand might —"

"Naow then there, Naow then!" suddenly came from the door in a hoarse cockney accent.

47

Flossie: a Venus of fifteen

"You jest let the lydy be, or oi'll give yer somethink to tyke' ome to yer dinner, see if oi don't!"

"Who is this person?" I asked of Eva, placing my hands upon her two breasts as if to shield them from the intruder's eye.

"Person yerself!" said the voice, "Fust thing *you've* a-got ter do is ter leave' old of my donah's breasties and then oi'll *tork* to ver!"

"But the lady has hurt herself, sir, and was consulting me professionally."

There was a moment's pause, during which I had time to examine my opponent when I found to be wearing a red Tam-o'-Shanter cap, a close fitting knitted silk blouse, a short white flannel skirt, and scarlet stockings. This charming figure threw itself upon me open-armed and open-mouthed and kissed me with delightful abandon.

After a hearty laugh over the success of Flossie's latest 'impersonation', Eva pushed us both out of the room, saying. "Take her away, Jack, and see if *she* has got any marks. Those bicycle saddles are rather trying sometimes. We will lunch in a quarter of an hour."

I bore my darling little mistress away to her room, and having helped her to strip off her clothes, I inspected on my knees the region

48

"How Flossie acquired the French tongue"

where the saddle might have been expected to gall her, but found nothing but a fair expanse of firm white bottom which I saluted with many lustful kisses upon every spot within reach of my tongue. Then I took her naked to the bathroom, and sponged her from neck to ankles, dried her thoroughly, just plunged my tongue once into her cunt, carried her back to her room, dressed her and presented her to Eva within twenty minutes of our leaving the latter's bedroom.

Below in the coffee-room, a capitally served luncheon awaited us. The table was laid in a sort of little annex to the principal room, and I was glad of the retirement, since we were able to enjoy to the full the constant flow of fun and mimicry with which Flossie brought tears of laughter to our eyes throughout the meal. Eva, too, was gifted with a fine sense of the ridiculous, and as I myself was at least an appreciative audience, the ball was kept rolling with plenty of spirit.

After lunch Eva announced her intention of going to a concert in Piccadilly, and a few minutes later Flossie and I were once more alone.

"Jack," she said, "I feel thoroughly and hopelessly naughty this afternoon. If you like I

49

Flossie: a Venus of fifteen

will go on with my story while you lie on the sofa and smoke a cigar."

This exactly suited my views and I said so.

"Very well, then. First give me a great big kiss with all the tongue you've got about you. Ah! that was good! Now I'm going to sit on this footstool beside you, and I *think* one or two of these buttons might be unfastened, so that I can feel whether the story is producing any effect upon you. Good gracious! why, it's as hard and stiff as a poker already. I really *must* frig it a little —"

"Quite gently and slowly then, *please* Flossie, or —"

"Yes, quite, *quite* gently and slowly, so — Is that nice, Jack?"

"Nice is not the word, darling!"

"Talking of words, Jack, I am afraid I shall hardly be able to finish my adventures without occasionally using a word or two which you don't hear at a Sunday School Class. Do you mind, very much? Of course you can always go and look out of the window, can't you!"

"My dearest little sweetheart, when we are alone together like this, and both feeling extremely naughty, as we do now, any and every word that comes from your dear lips sounds sweet and utterly void of offence to me."

"How Flossie acquired the French tongue"

"Very well, then; that makes it ever so much easier to tell my story, and if I *should* become too shocking — well, you know how I love you to stop my mouth, don't you Jack!"

A responsive throb from my imprisoned member gave her all the answer she required.

"Let me see," she began, "where was I? Oh, I remember, in Ylette's bed."

"Yes, she had gamahuched you, and you were just performing the same friendly office for her."

"Of course: I was telling you how the length of my tongue made up for the shortness of my experience, or so Ylette was kind enough to say. I think she meant it too: at any rate she spent several times before I gave up my position between her legs. After this we tried the double gamahuche, which proved a great success because, although she was, as I have told you, two years older than I, we were almost exactly of a height, so that as she knelt over me, her cunt came quite naturally upon my mouth, and her mouth upon my cunt, and in this position we were able to give each other an enormous amount of pleasure."

At this point I was obliged to beg Flossie to remove her right hand from the situation it was occupying.

"What I cannot understand about it," she

51

Flossie: a Venus of fifteen

went on, "is that there are any number of girls in France, and a good many in England too, who after they have once been gamahuched by another girl don't care about anything else. Perhaps it means that they have never been really in love with a man, because to *me* one touch of your lips in that particular neighbourhood is worth ten thousand kisses from anybody else, male or female and when I have got your dear, darling, delicious prick in my mouth, I want nothing else in the whole wide world, except to give you the greatest possible amount of pleasure and to make you spend down my throat in the quickest possible time —"

"If you really want to beat the record, Flossie, I think there's a good chance now —"

Almost before the words had passed my lips the member in question was between *hers*, where it soon throbbed to the crisis in response to the indescribable sucking action of mouth and tongue of which she possessed the secret.

On my telling her how exquisite were the sensations she procured me by this means she replied:

"Oh, you have to thank Ylette for that! Just before we became friends she had gone for the long holidays to a country house belonging to a young couple who were great friends of hers.

52

"How Flossie acquired the French tongue"

There was a very handsome boy of eighteen or so staying in the house. He fell desperately in love with Ylette and she with him, and he taught her exactly how to gamahuche him so as to produce the utmost amount of pleasure. As she told me afterwards, "Every day, every night, almost ever hour, he would bury his prick in my mouth, frig it against my tongue, and fill my throat with a divine flood. With a charming amiability, he worked incessantly to shew me every kind of gamahuching, all the possible ways of sucking a man's prick. Nothing, said he, should be left to the imagination, which, he explained, can never produce such good results as a few practical lessons given in detail upon a real standing prick, plunged to the very root in the mouth of the girl pupil, to whom one can thus describe on the spot the various suckings, hard, soft, slow or quick, of which it is essential she should know the precise effect in order to obtain the quickest and most copious flow of the perfumed liquor which she desires to draw from her lover."

"I suppose," Ylette went on, "that one invariably likes what one can do well. Anyhow, my greatest pleasure in life is to suck a goodlooking boy's prick. If he likes to slip his tongue into my cunt at the same time, *tant mieux.*"

Flossie: a Venus of fifteen

"Unfortunately this delightful boy could only stay a fortnight, but as there were several other young men of the party, and as her lover was wise enough to know that after his recent lessons in the art of love, Ylette could not be expected to be an abstainer, he begged her to enjoy herself in his absence, with the result, as she said that 'au bout d'une semaine il n'y avait pas un vit dans la maison qui ne m'avait tripoté la luette (I), ni une langue qui n'était l'amie intime de mon con.'

"Every one of these instructions Ylette passed on to me, with practical illustrations upon my second finger standing as substitute for the real thing, which, of course, was not to be had in the school at — least not just then.

"She must have been an excellent teacher, for I have never had any other lessons than hers, and yours is the first and only staff of love that I have ever had the honour of gamahuching. However, I mean to make up now for lost time, for I would have you to know, my darling, that I am madly in love with every bit of your body, and that most of all do I adore your angel prick with its coral head that I so love to suck and

---

*) Uvula

"How Flossie acquired the French tongue"

plunge into my mouth. Come, Jack, Come! let us have one more double gamahuche. One moment! There! Now I am naked. I am going to kneel over your face with my legs wide apart and my cunt kissing your mouth. Drive the whole of your tongue into it, won't you, Jack, and make it curl round my clitoris. Yes! that's it — just like that. Lovely! Now I can't talk any more, because I am going to fill my mouth with the whole of your darling prick; push; push it down my throat, Jack, and when the time comes, spend your very longest and most. I'm going to frig you a little first and rub you under your balls. Goodness! how the dear thing is standing. In he goes now ... m ... m ... m ... m ... m ... m ... "

A few inarticulate gasps and groans of pleasure were the only sounds audible for some minutes during which each strove to render the sensations of the other as acute as possible. I can answer for it that Flossie's success was complete, and by the convulsive movements of her bottom and the difficulty I experienced in keeping the position of my tongue upon her palpitating clitoris, I gathered that my operations had not altogether failed of their object. In this I was confirmed by the copious and protracted discharge which the beloved cunt delivered into my

55

Flossie: a Venus of fifteen

throat at the same instant as the incomparable mouth received my yard to the very root, and a perfect torrent rewarded her delicious efforts for my enjoyment.

"Ah, Jack! that was just heavenly," she sighed, as she rose from her charming position. "*How* you did spend, that time, you darling old boy, and so did I, eh, Jack?"

"My little angel, I thought you would never have finished," I replied.

"Do you know, Jack, I believe you really did get a little way down my throat, then! At any rate you managed the 'tripotage de luette' that Ylette's friend recommended so strongly!"

"And I don't think I ever got quite so far into your cunt, Flossie."

"That's quite true; I felt your tongue touch a spot it had never reached before. And just wasn't it lovely when you got there! It almost makes me spend again to think of it! But I am not going to be naughty any more. And to show you how truly virtuous I am feeling, I'll continue my story if you like. I want to get on with it, because I know you must be wondering all the time how a person of my age can have come to be so . . . what shall we say, Jack?"

"Larky," I suggested.

"Yes, 'larky' will do. Of course I have always

56

"How Flossie acquired the French tongue"

been 'older than my age' as the saying goes, and my friendship with Ylette and all the lovely things she used to do to me made me 'come on' much faster than most girls. I ought to tell you that I got to be rather a favourite at school, and after it came to be known that Ylette and I were on gamahuching terms, I used to get little notes from almost every girl in the school over twelve, imploring me to sleep with her. One dear little thing even went so far as to give me the measurements of her tongue, which she had taken with a piece of string."

"Oh, I say, Flossie, *come now* — I can swallow a good deal but — "

"You can indeed, Jack, as I have good reason to know! But all the same it's absolutely true. You can't have any conception what French school-girls of fourteen or fifteen are. There is nothing they won't do to get themselves gamahuched, and if a girl is pretty or fascinating or has particularly good legs, or specially large breasts, she may, if she likes, have a fresh admirer's head under her petticoats every day in the week. Of course, it's all very wrong and dreadful, I know, but what else can you expect? In France gamahuching between grown-up men and women is a recognised thing — "

"Not only in France, *nowadays*," I put in.

57

Flossie: a Venus of fifteen

"So I have heard. But at any rate in France every body does it. Girls at school naturally know this, as they know most things. At that time of life — at *my* time of life, if you like — a girl thinks and dreams of nothing else. She cannot, except by some extraordinary luck, find herself alone with a boy or man. One day her girl chum at school pops her head under her petticoats and gamahuches her deliciously. How can you wonder if from that moment she is ready to go through fire and water to obtain the same pleasure?"

"Go on, Flossie. You are simply delicious to-day!"

"Don't laugh, Jack. I am very serious about it. I don't care how much a girl of (say) my age longs for a boy to be naughty with — it's perfectly right and natural. What I think is bad is that she should *begin* by having a liking for a girl's tongue inculcated into her. I should like to see boys and girls turned loose upon one another once a week or so at authorized gamahuching parties, which should be attended by masters and governesses (who would have to see that the *other* thing was not indulged in, of course). Then the girls would grow up with a good healthy taste for the other sex, and even if they did do a little gamahuching amongst them-

"How Flossie acquired the French tongue"

selves between whiles, it would only be to keep themselves going till the next 'party'. By my plan a boy's prick would be the central object of their desires, as it ought to be. Now *I* think that's a very fine scheme, Jack, and as soon as I am a little older, I shall go to Paris and put it before the Minister of Education!"

"But why wait, Flossie? Why not go now?"

"Well, you see, if the old gentleman (I suppose he is old, isn't he, or he wouldn't be a minister?) — if he saw a girl in short frocks, he would think she had got some private object to serve in regard to the gamahuching parties. Whereas a grown-up person who had plainly left school might be supposed to be doing it unselfishly for the good of the rising generation."

"Yes, I understand that. But when you *do* go, Flossie, please take me or some other respectable person with you, because I don't altogether trust that Minister of Education and whatever the length of your frocks might happen to be at the time, I feel certain that, old or young, the moment you had explained your noble scheme, he would be wanting some practical illustrations on the office arm-chair!"

"How dare you suggest such a thing, Jack! You are to understand, sir, that from henceforth my mouth is reserved for three purposes, to eat

59

Flossie: a Venus of fifteen

with, to talk with, and to kiss you with on whatever part of your person I may happen to fancy at the moment. By the way, you won't mind my making just one exception in favour of Eva, will you? She loves me to make her nipples stand with my tongue; occasionally, too we perform the *'soixant neuf'*."

"When the next performance takes place, may I be there to see?" I ejaculated fervently.

"Oh, Jack, how shocking!"

"Does it shock you, Flossie? Very well, then I withdraw it, and apologise."

"You cannot withdraw it now. You have distinctly stated that you would like to be there when Eva and I have our next gamahuche."

"Well, I suppose I *did* say."

"Silence, sir," said Flossie in a voice of thunder, and shaking her brown head at me with inexpressible ferocity. "You have made a proposal of the most indecent character, and the sentence of the Court is that, at the first possible opportunity, you shall be *held to that proposal!* Meanwhile the Court condemns you to receive 250 kisses on various parts of your body, which it will at once proceed to administer. Now, sir, off with your clothes!"

"Mayn't I keep my . . . "

"No, sir, you may *not!*"

60

"How Flossie acquired the French tongue"

The sentence of the Court was accordingly carried out to the letter, somewhere about three-fourths of the kisses being applied upon one and the same part of the prisoner to which the Court attached its mouth with extraordinary gusto.

CHAPTER III

Nox Ambrosiana

MY INTERCOURSE WITH THE TENANTS OF THE flat became daily more intimate and more frequent. My love for Flossie grew intensely deep and strong as opportunities increased for observing the rare sweetness and amiability of her character, and the charm which breathed like a spell over everything she said and did. At one moment, so great was her tact and so keen her judgment, I would find myself consulting her on a knotty point with the certainty of getting sound advice; at another the child in her would suddenly break out and she would romp and play about like the veriest kitten. Then there would be yet another reaction, and without a word of warning, she would become amorous and caressing and seizing upon her favourite plaything, would push it into her mouth and suck it in a perfect frenzy of erotic passion. It is hardly necessary to say that these contrasts of mood lent an infinite zest to our liaison and I had al-

Flossie: a Venus of fifteen

most ceased to long for its more perfect consummation. But one warm June evening, allusion was again made to the subject by Flossie, who repeated her sorrow for the deprivation she declared I must be feeling so greatly.

I assured her that it was not so.

"Well, Jack, if you aren't, *I* am," she cried. "And what is more there is some one else who is 'considerably likewise' as our old gardener used to say."

"What *do* you mean, child?"

She darted into the next room and came back almost directly.

"Sit down there and listen to me. In that room, lying asleep on her bed, is the person whom, after you, I love best in the world. There is nothing I wouldn't do for her, and I'm sure you'll believe this when I tell you that I am going to beg you on my knees, to go in there and do to Eva what my promise to her prevents me from letting you do to me. Now, Jack, I know you love me and you know *dearly* I love you. Nothing can alter *that*. Well, Jack, if you will go into Eva, gamahuche her well and let her gamahuche you (she *adores* it), and then have her thoroughly and in all positions — I shall simply love you a thousand times better than ever."

64

Nox Ambrosiana

"But Flossie, my darling, Eva doesn't —"

"Oh, doesn't she! Wait till you get between her legs, and see! Come along: I'll just put you inside the room and then leave you. She is lying outside her bed for coolness — on her side. Lie down quietly *behind* her. She will be almost sure to think it's me, and perhaps you will hear — something interesting. Quick's the word! Come!"

The sight which met my eyes on entering Eva's bedroom was enough to take one's breath away. She lay on her side, with her face towards the door, stark naked, and fast asleep. I crept noiselessly towards her and gazed upon her glorious nudity in speechless delight. Her dark hair fell in a cloud about her white shoulders. Her fine face was slightly flushed, the full red lips a little parted. Below, the gleaming breasts caught the light from the shaded lamp at her bedside, the pink nipples rising and falling to the time of her quiet breathing. One fair round arm was behind her head, the other lay along the exquisitely turned thigh. The good St. Antony might have been pardoned for owning himself defeated by such a picture!

As is usual with a sleeping person who is being looked at, Eva stirred a little, and her lips

Flossie: a Venus of fifteen

opened as if to speak. I moved on tiptoe to the other side of the bed, and stripping myself naked, lay down beside her.

Then, without turning round, a sleepy voice said, "Ah, Flossie, are you there? What have you done with Jack? *(a pause)*. When are you going to lend him to me for a night, Flossie? I wish I'd got him here now, between my legs — betwe-e-e-n m-y-y-y le-egs! Oh dear! how randy I do feel to-night. When I *do* have Jack for a night, Flossie, may I take his prick in my mouth before we do the other thing? Flossie — Floss*ee* — why don't you answer? Little darling! I expect she's tired out, and no wonder! Well, I suppose I'd better put something on me and go to sleep too!"

As she raised herself from the pillow, her hand came in contact with my person.

"Angels and Ministers of Grace defend us! What's this? *You*, Jack! *And you've heard what I've been saying?*"

"I'm afraid I have, Eva."

"Well, it doesn't matter: I meant it all, and more besides! Now before I do anything else I simply must run in and kiss that darling Floss for sending you to me. It is just like her, and I can't say anything stronger than *that!*"

"Jack," she said on coming back to the room.

66

Nox Ambrosiana

"I warn you that you are going to have a stormy night. In the matter of love, I've gone starving for many months. To-night I'm fairly roused, and when in that state, I believe I am about the most erotic bed-fellow to be found anywhere. Flossie has given me leave to *say* and do anything and everything to you, and I mean to use the permission for all its worth. Flossie tells me that you are an absolutely perfect gamahucher. Now I adore being gamahuched. Will you do that for me, Jack?"

"My dear girl, I should rather think so!"

"Good! But it is not to be all on one side. I shall gamahuche you, too, and you will have to own that I know something of the art. Another thing you may perhaps like to try is what the French call *'fouterie aux seins'*."

"I know all about it, and if I may insert monsieur Jacques between those magnificent breasts of yours, I shall die of the pleasure."

"Good again. Now we come to the legitimate drama, from which you and Floss have so nobly abstained. I desire to be thoroughly and comprehensively fucked to-night — sorry to have to use the word, Jack, but it is the only one that expresses my meaning."

"Don't apologise, dear. Under present circumstances all words are allowable."

67

Flossie: a Venus of fifteen

"Glad to hear you say that, because it makes conversation so much easier. Now let me take hold of your prick, and frig it a little, so that I may judge what size it attains in full erection. So! he's a fine boy, and I think he will fit my cunt to a turn. I must kiss his pretty head, it looks so tempting. Ah! delicious! See here Jack, I will lie back with my head on the pillow, and you shall just come and kneel over me and have me in the mouth. Push away gaily, just as if you were fucking me, and when you are going to spend, slip one hand under my neck and drive your prick down my throat, and do not *dare* to withdraw it until I have received all you have to give me. Sit upon my chest first for a minute and let me tickle your prick with the nipples of my breasts. Is that nice? Ah! I knew you would like it! *Now* kneel up to my face, and I will suck you."

With eagerly pouting lips and clutching fingers, she seized upon my straining yard, and pressed it into her soft mouth. Arrived there, it was saluted by the velvet tongue which twined itself about the nut in a thousand lascivious motions.

Mindful of Eva's instructions, I began to work the instrument as if it was in another place. At

Nox Ambrosiana

once she laid her hands upon my buttocks and regulated the time of my movements, assisting them by a corresponding action of her head. Once, owing to carelessness on my part, her lips lost their hold altogether; with a little cry, she caught my prick in her fingers and in an instant, it was again between her lips and revelling in the adorable pleasure of their sucking.

A moment later and my hands were under her neck, for the signal, and my very soul seemed to be exhaled from me in response to the clinging of her mouth as she felt my prick throb with the passage of love's torrent.

After a minute's rest, and a word of gratitude for the transcendent pleasure she had given me, I began a tour of kisses over the enchanting regions which lay between her neck and her knees, ending with a protracted sojourn in the most charming spot of all. As I approached this last, she said.

"Please to begin by passing your tongue slowly round the edges of the lips, then thrust it into the lower part at full length and keep it there working it in and out for a little. Then move it gradually up to the top and when there, press your tongue firmly against my clitoris a minute or so. Next take the clitoris between your lips and suck it *furiously*, bite it gently, and slip the

69

Flossie: a Venus of fifteen

point of your tongue underneath it. When I have spent twice, which I am sure to do in the first three minutes, get up and lie between my legs, drive the whole of your tongue into my mouth, and the whole of your prick into my cunt, and fuck me with all your might and main!"

I could not resist a smile at the naiveté of these circumstantial directions. My amusement was not lost upon Eva, who hastened to explain, by reminding me again that it was "ages" since she had been touched by a man. "In gamahuching," she said, "the *details* are everything. In copulation they are not so important, since the principal things that increase one's enjoyment — such as the quickening of the stroke towards the end by the man, and the knowing exactly how and when to apply the *nipping* action of the cunt by the woman — come more or less naturally, especially with practice. But now, Jack, I want to be gamahuched, please."

"And I'm longing to be at you, dear. Come and kneel astride of me, and let me kiss your cunt without any more delay."

Eva was pleased to approve of this position and in another moment, I was slipping my tongue into the delicious cavity which opened wider and wider to receive its caresses, and to

Nox Ambrosiana

enable it to plunge further and further into the perfumed depths. My attentions were next turned to the finely developed clitoris which I found to be extraordinarily sensitive. In fact, Eva's own time limit of three minutes had not been reached, when the second effusion escaped her, and a third was easily obtained by a very few more strokes of the tongue. After this, she laid herself upon her back, drew me towards her and, taking hold of my prick, placed it tenderly between her breasts, and pressing them together with her hands, urged me to enjoy myself in this enchanting position. The length and stiffness imparted to my member by the warmth and softness of her breasts delighted her beyond measure, and she implored me to fuck her without any further delay. I was never more ready or better furnished than at that moment, and after she had once more taken my prick into her mouth for a moment, I slipped down to the desired position between her thighs which she had already parted to their uttermost to receive me. In an instant she had guided the staff of love to the exact spot, and with a heave of her bottom, aided by an answering thrust from me, had buried it to the root within the soft of its natural covering.

Nox Ambrosiana

Eva's description of herself as an erotic bedfellow had hardly prepared me for the joys I was to experience in her arms. From the moment the nut of my yard touched her womb, she became as one possessed. Her eyes were turned heavenwards, her tongue twined round my own in rapture, her hands played about my body, now clasping my neck, now working feverishly up and down my back, and ever and again, creeping down to her lower parts where her first and second finger would rest compassshaped upon the two edges of her cunt, pressing themselves upon my prick as it glided in and out and adding still further to the maddening pleasure I was undergoing. Her breath came in short quick gasps, the calve of her legs sometimes lay upon my own but more often were locked over my loins or buttocks, thus enabling her to time to a nicety the strokes of my body, and to respond with accurately judged thrusts from her own splendid bottom. At last a low musical cry came from her parted lips, she strained me to her naked body with redoubled fury and driving the whole length of her tongue into my mouth, she spent long and deliciously, whilst I flooded her clinging cunt with a torrent of unparalleled volume and duration.

Nox Ambrosiana

"Jack," she whispered, "I have never enjoyed anything half so much in my life before. I hope you liked it too?"

"I don't think you can expect anyone to say that he "liked" fucking *you*, Eva! One might 'like' kissing your hand, or helping you on with an opera cloak or some minor pleasure of that sort. But to lie between a pair of legs like yours, cushioned on a pair of breasts like yours, with a tongue like yours down one's throat, and one's prick held in the soft grip of a cunt like yours, is to undergo a series of sensations such as don't come twice in a lifetime."

Eva's eyes flashed as she gathered me closer in her naked arms and said.

"*Don't* they, though! In this particular instance I am going to see that they come twice *within half an hour!*"

"Well, I've come twice in less than half an hour and —"

"Oh! I know what you are going to say, but we'll soon put that all right."

A careful examination of the state of affairs was then made by Eva who bent her pretty head for the purpose, kneeling on the bed in a position which enabled me to gaze at my leisure upon all her secret charms.

Her operations meanwhile were causing me

Flossie: a Venus of fifteen

exquisite delight. With an indescribable tenderness of action, soft and caressing as that of a young mother tending her sick child, she slipped the fingers of her left hand under my balls while the other hand wandered luxuriously over the surrounding country and finally came to an anchor upon my prick, which not unnaturally began to show signs of returning vigour. Pleased at the patient's improved state of health, she passed her delicious velvet tongue up and down and round and into a standing position! This sudden and satisfactory result of her ministrations so excited her that, without letting go of her prisoner, she cleverly passed one leg over me as I lay, and behold us in the traditional attitude of the *gamahuche a deux!* I now, for the first time, looked upon Eva's cunt in its full beauty, and I gladly devoted a moment to the inspection before plunging my tongue between the rich red lips which seemed to kiss my mouth as it clung in ecstasy to their luscious folds. I may say here that in point of colour, proportion and beauty of outline, Eva Letchford's cunt was the most perfect I had ever seen or gamahuched, though in after years my darling little Flossie's displayed equal faultlessness, and, as being the cunt of my beloved little sweetheart, whom I adored, it was entitled to and received

Nox Ambrosiana

from me a degree of homage never accorded to any other before or since.

The particular part of my person to which Eva was paying attention soon attained in her mouth a size and hardness which did the highest credit to her skill. With my tongue revelling in its enchanted resting-place, and my prick occupying what a house-agent might truth fully describe as "this most desirable site," I was personally content to remain as we were, whilst Eva, entirely abandoning herself to her charming occupation, had apparently forgotten the object with which she had originally undertaken it. Fearing therefore lest the clinging mouth and delicately twining tongue should bring about the crisis which Eva had designed should take place elsewhere, I reluctantly took my lips from the clitoris they were enclosing at the moment, and called to its owner to stop.

"But Jack, you're just going to spend!" was the plaintive reply.

"Exactly, dear! And how about the 'twice in half an hour'."

"Oh! of course. You were going to fuck me again, weren't you! Well, you'll find Massa Johnson in pretty good trim for the fray," and she laughingly held up my prick, which was really of enormous dimensions, and plunging it

Flossie: a Venus of fifteen

downwards let it rebound with a loud report against my belly.

This appeared to delight her, for she repeated it several times. Each time the elasticity seemed to increase and the force of the recoil to become greater.

"The darling!" she cried, as she kissed the coral head. "He is going to his own chosen abiding place. Come! Come! Come! blessed, *blessed* prick. Bury yourself in this loving cunt which longs for you; frig yourself deliciously against the lips which wait to kiss you; plunge into the womb which yearns to receive your life-giving seed; pause as you go by to press the clitoris that loves you. Come, divine, adorable prick! fuck me, fuck me, fuck me! fuck me long and hard: fuck and spare not! — Jack, you are into me, my cunt clings to your prick, do you feel how it nips you? Push, Jack, further; now your balls are kissing my bottom. That's lovely! Crush my breasts with your chest, *cr-r-r-r-ush* them, Jack. Now go slowly a moment, and let your prick gently rub my clitoris. So . . . o . . o . . . Now faster and harder . . . faster still — now your tongue in my mouth, and dig your nails into my bottom. I'm going to spend: fuck, Jack, fuck me, fuck me, fu-u-u-uck me! Heavens! what bliss it is! Ah you're spending too

76

Nox Ambrosiana

bo . . . o . . . o . . . oth together, both toge . . . e e . . . ther. Pour it into me, Jack! Flood me, drown me, fill my womb. God! What rapture. Don't stop. Your prick is still hard and long. Drive it into me — touch my navel. Let me get my hand down to frig you as you go in and out. The sweet prick! He's stiffer than ever. How splendid of him! Fuck me again. Jack. Ah! fuck me till to-morrow, fuck me till I die."

I fear that this language in the cold form of print may seem more than a little crude. Yet those who have experience of a beautiful and refined woman, abandoning herself in moments of passion to similar freedom of speech, will own the stimulus thus given to the sexual powers. In the present instance its effect, joined to the lascivious touches and never ceasing efforts to arouse and increase desire of this deliciously lustful girl, was to impart an unprecedented stiffness to my member which throbbed almost to bursting within the enclosing cunt and pursued its triumphant career to such lengths, that even the resources of the insatiable Eva gave out at last, and she lay panting in my arms, where soon afterwards she passed into a quiet sleep. Drawing a silken coverlet over her, I rose with great caution, slipped on my clothes, and in five minutes was on my way home.

CHAPTER IV

More of Flossie's school-life; and other matters

"Good morning, Captain Archer, I trust that you have slept well?" said Flossie on my presenting myself at the flat early the next day. "My friend Miss Letchford," she went on, in a prim middleaged tone of voice, "has not yet left her apartment. She complains of having passed a somewhat disturbed night owing to — ahem!"

"Rats in the wainscot?" I suggested.

"No, my friend attributes her sleepless condition to a severe irritation in the — forgive the immodesty of my words — lower part of her person, followed by a prolonged pricking in the same region. She is still feeling the effects, and I found her violently clasping a pillow between her — ahem! — legs, which which she was apparently endeavouring to soothe her feelings."

"Dear me! Miss Eversley, do you think I could

79

Flossie: a Venus of fifteen

be of any assistance?" *(stepping towards Eva's door.)*

"You are *most* kind, Captain Archer, but I have already done what I could in the way of friction and — other little attentions, which left the poor sufferer somewhat calmer. Now, Jack, you wretch! you haven't kissed me yet . . . That's better! You will not be surprised to hear that Eva has given me a full and detailed description of her sleepless night, in her own language, which I have no doubt you have discovered, is just a bit *graphic* at times."

"Well, my little darling, I did my best, as I knew you would wish me to do. It wasn't difficult with such a bed-fellow as Eva. But charming and amorous as she is, I couldn't help feeling all the time 'if it were only my little Flossie lying under me now!' By the way how utterly lovely you are this morning, Floss."

She was dressed in a short sprigged cotton frock, falling very little below her knees, shot pink and black stockings, and low patent leather shoes with silver buckles. Her long waving brown hair gleamed gold in the morning light, and the deep blue eyes glowed with health and love, and now and again flashed with merri-

80

More of Flossie's school-life

ment. I gazed upon her in rapture at her beauty.

"Do you like my frock, Jack? I'm glad. It's the first time I've had it on. It's part of my trousseau."

"Your *what*, Flossie?" I shouted.

"I said my trousseau," she repeated quietly, but with sparks of fun dancing in her sweet eyes. "The fact is, Jack, Eva declared the other day that though I am not married to you, you and I are really on a sort of honeymoon. So, as I have just had a good lot of money from the lawyers, she made me go with her and buy everything new. Look here," *(unfastening her bodice)* "new stays, new chemise, new stockings and oh! Jack, *look!* such *lovely* new drawers — none of your horrid vulgar knickerbockers, trimmings and lovely little tucks all the way up, and quite wide open in front for . . . ventilation I suppose! Feel what soft stuff they are made of! Eva was awfully particular about these drawers. She is always so practical, you know."

"Practical!" I interrupted.

"Yes. What she said was that you would often be wanting to kiss me between my legs when there wasn't time to undress and be naked together, so that I must have drawers made of

81

Flossie: a Venus of fifteen

the finest and most delicate stuff to please you, and with the opening cut extra wide so as not to get in the way of your tongue! Now don't you call that practical?"

"I do indeed! Blessed Eva, that's another good turn I owe her!"

"Well, for instance, there isn't time to undress *now*, Jack, and —"

She threw herself back in her chair and in an instant, I had plunged under the short rose-scented petticoats and had my mouth glued to the beloved cunt once more. In the midst of the delicious operation, I fancied I heard a slight sound from the direction of Eva's door and just then, Flossie locked her hands behind my head and pressed me to her with even more than her usual ardour; a moment later deluging my throat with the perfumed essence of her being.

You darling old boy, how you *did* make me spend that time! I really think your tongue is longer than it was. Perhaps the warmth of Eva's interior has made it grow! Now I must be off to the dressmaker's for an hour or so. By the way, she wants to make my frocks longer. She declares people can see my drawers when I run upstairs."

"Don't you let her do it, Floss."

More of Flossie's school-life

"*Rather not!* What's the use of buying expensive drawers like mine if you can't show them to a pal! *Good* morning, Captain! Sorry I can't stop. While I'm gone you might just step in and see how my lydy friend's gettin' on. Fust door on the right. *Good* morning!"

For a minute or two, I lay back in my chair and wondered whether I would not take my hat and go. But a moments' further reflection told me that I must do as Flossie directed me. To this decision, I must own, the memory of last night's pleasure and the present demands of a most surprising erection contributed in no small degree. Accordingly, I tapped at Eva's bedroom door.

She had just come from her bath and wore only a peignoir and her stockings. On seeing me, she at once let fall her garment and stood before me in radiant nakedness.

"Look at this", she said, holding out a half-sheet of notepaper. "I found it on my pillow when I woke an hour ago.

" 'If Jack comes this morning I shall send him in to see you while I go to Virginie's. Let him — *anything beginning with "f" or "s" that rhymes with* luck — you.' "A hair of the dog",

83

Flossie: a Venus of fifteen

etc., will do you both good. My time will come. Ha! Ha!"

"Floss."

"Now I ask you, Jack, was there ever such an adorable little darling?"

My answer need not be recorded.

Eva came close to me and thrust her hand inside my clothes.

"Ah! I see you are of the same way of thinking as myself," she said taking hold of my fingers and carrying them on her cunt, which pouted hungrily. "So let us have one good royal fuck and then you can stay here with me while I dress, and I'll tell you anything that Flossie may have left out about her school-life in Paris. Will that meet your views?"

"Exactly," I replied.

"Very well then. As we are going to limit ourselves to *one*, would you mind fucking me *en levrette?*"

"Any way you like, most puissant and fucksome of ladies!"

I stripped off my clothes in a twinkling and Eva placed herself in position, standing on the rug and bending forwards with her elbows on the bed. I reverently saluted the charms thus

84

More of Flossie's school-life

presented to my lips, omitting none, and then rising from my knees, advanced, weapon in hand, to storm the breach. As I approached, Eva opened her legs to their widest extent, and I drove my straining prick into the mellow cunt, fucking it with unprecedented vigour and delight, as the lips alternately parted and contracted, nipping me with an extraordinary force in response to the pressure of my right forefinger upon the clitoris and of my left upon the nipples of the heaving breasts. Keen as was the enjoyment we were both experiencing the fuck — as in invariably the case with a morning performance — was of very protacted duration, and several minutes had elapsed before I dropped my arms to Eva's thighs and, with my belly glued against her bottom and my face nestling between her shoulder blades, felt the rapturous throbbing of my prick as it discharged an avalanche into the innermost recesses of her womb.

"Don't move, Jack, for Heaven's sake," she cried.

"Don't want to, Eva, I'm quite happy where I am, thank you!"

Moving an inch or two further out from the bed so as to give herself more "play", she

85

Flossie: a Venus of fifteen

started an incredibly provoking motion of her bottom, so skilfully executed that it produced the impression of being almost *spiral*. The action is difficult to describe, but her bottom rose and fell, moved backward and forward, and from side to side in quick alternation, the result being that my member was constantly in contact with, as it were, some fresh portion of the embracing cunt, the soft folds of which seemed by their varied and tender caresses to be pleading to him to emerge from his present state of partial apathy and resume the proud condition he had displayed before.

"Will he come up this way, Jack, or shall I take the dear little man in my mouth and suck him into an erection?"

"I think he'll be all right as he is, dear. Just keep on nipping him with your cunt and push your bottom a little closer to me so that I may feel your naked flesh against mine . . . *that's* it!"

"Ah! the darling prick, he's beginning to swell! he's going to fuck me directly, I know he is! Your finger on my cunt in front, please Jack, and the other hand on my nipples. So! *that's* nice. Oh dear! how I *do* want your tongue in my mouth, but that can't be. Now begin and

More of Flossie's school-life

fuck me slowly at first. Your *second* finger on my clitoris, please, and frig me in time to the motion of your body. Now fuck faster a little, and deeper into me. Push, dear, push like a demon. Pinch my nipple; a little faster on the clitoris. I'm spending! I'm dying of delight! Fuck me, Jack, keep on fucking me. Don't be afraid. Strike against my bottom with all your strength, harder still, harder! Now put your hands down to my thighs and *drag* me on to you. Lovely! grip the flesh of my thighs with your fingers and fuck me to the very womb."

"Eva, look out! I'm going to spend!"

"So am I, Jack. Ah! how your prick throbs against my cunt! Fuck me, Jack, to the last moment, spend your last drop, as I'm doing. One last push up to the hilt — there, keep him in like that and let me have a deluge from you. How exquisite! how adorable to spend together! *One* moment more before you take him out, and let me kiss him with my cunt before I say good-bye."

"What a nip that was, Eva, it felt more like a hand on me than a —"

"Yes", she interrupted, turning round and facing me with her eyes languorous and velvety with lust, "that is my only accomplishment, and I must say I think it's a valuable one! In Paris

87

Flossie: a Venus of fifteen

I had a friend — but no matter I'm not going to talk about myself, but about Flossie. Sit down in that chair, and have a cigarette while I talk to you. I'm going to stay naked if you don't mind. It's so hot. Now if you're quite comfy, I'll begin."

She seated herself opposite to me, her splendid naked body full in the light from the window near her.

"There is a part of Flossie's school story," began Eva, "which she has rather shrunk from telling you, and so I propose to relate the incident, in which I am sure you will be sufficiently interested. For the first twelve months of her school days in Paris, nothing very special occured to her beyond the cementing of her friendship with Ylette Vespertin. Flossie was a tremendous favourite with the other girls on account of her sweet nature and her extraordinary beauty, and there is no doubt that a great many curly heads were popped under her petticoats at one time and another. All these heads, however, belonged to her own sex, and no great harm was done. But at last there arrived at the convent a certain Camille de Losgrain, who, though by no means averse to the delights of gamahuche, nursed a strong preference for

88

More of Flossie's school-life

male, as against female charms. Camille speedily struck up an alliance with a handsome boy of seventeen who lived in the house next door. This youth had often seen Flossie and greatly desired her acquaintance. It seems that his bedroom window was on the same level as that of the room occupied by Flossie, Camille and three other girls, all of whom knew him by sight and had severally expressed a desire to have him between their legs. So it was arranged one night that he was to climb on to a buttress below his room, and the girls would manage to haul him into theirs. All this had to be done in darkness, as of course no light could be shewn. The young gentleman duly arrived on the scene in safety — the two eldest girls divested him of his clothes, and then, according to previous agreement, the five damsels sat naked on the edge of the bed in the pitch dark room, and Master Don Juan was to decide, by passing his hands over their bodies, which of the five should be favoured with his attentions. No one was to speak, to touch his person or to make any sign of interest. Twice the youth essayed this novel kind of ordeal by touch, and after a moment's profound silence he said, 'J'ai choisi, c'est la troisieme.' 'La troisieme' was no other than Flossie, the size of whose breasts had at

89

Flossie: a Venus of fifteen

once attracted him as well as given a clue to her identity. And now, Jack, I hope the sequel will not distress you. The other girls accepted the decision most loyally, having no doubt anticipated it. They laid Flossie tenderly on the bed and lavished every kind of caress upon her, gamahuching her with especial tenderness, so as to open the road as far as possible to the invader. It fortunately turned out to be the case that the boy's prick was not by any means of abnormal size, and as the dear little maidenhead had been already subjected to very considerable wear and tear of fingers and tongues the entrance was, as she told me herself, effected with a minimum of pain and discomfort, hardly felt indeed in the midst of the frantic kisses upon mouth, eyes, nipples, breasts and buttocks which the four excited girls rained upon her throughout the operation. As for the boy, his enjoyment knew no bounds, and when his alloted time was up could hardly be persuaded to make the return voyage to his room. This, however, was at last accomplished, and the four virgins hastened to hear from their ravished friend the full true and particular account of her sensations. For several nights after this, the boy made his appearance in the room, where he fucked all the other four in

More of Flossie's school-life

succession, and pined openly for Flossie, who, however, regarded him as belonging to Camille and declined anything beyond the occasional service of his tongue which she greatly relished and which he, of course, as gladly put at her disposal.

"All this happened before my time and was related to me afterwards by Flossie herself. It is only just a year ago that I was engaged to teach English at the convent. Like everyone else who is brought in contact with her, I at once fell in love with Flossie and we quickly became the greatest of friends. Six months ago, came a change of fortune for me, an old bachelor uncle dying suddenly and leaving me a competence. By this time, the attachment between Flossie and myself had become so deep that the child could not bear the thought of parting from me. I too was glad enough of the excuse thus given for writing to Flossie's guardian — who has never taken more than a casual interest in her — to propose her returning to England with me and the establishment of a joint menage. My 'references' being satisfactory, and Flossie having declared herself to be most anxious for the plan, the guardian made no objection and in short — here we are!"

"Well, that's a very interesting story, Eva.

Flossie: a Venus of fifteen

Only — *confound* that French boy and his buttress!"

"Yes, you would naturally feel like that about it, and I don't blame you. Only you must remember that if it hadn't been for the size of Flossie's breasts, and its being done in the dark, and . . ."

"But Eva, you don't mean to tell me the young brute wouldn't have chosen her out of the five if there had been a *light*, do you!"

"No, of course not. What I *do* mean is that it was all a sort of fluke, and that Flossie is really, to all intents and purposes . . . "

"Yes, yes, I know what you would like to say, and I entirely and absolutely agree with you. I *love* Flossie with all my heart and soul and . . . well, that French boy can go to the devil!"

"Miss Eva! Niss Eva!" came a voice outside the door.

"Well, what is it?"

"Oh, if you please, Miss, there's a young man downstairs called for his little account. Says'e's the coals, Miss. I *towld* him you was engaged, Miss?"

"Did you — and what did he say?"

" 'Ow!' 'e sez, 'engeyged, *is* she', 'e sez — 'well, you tell'er from me confidential-like, as it's 'igh time she was *married*', 'e sez!"

92

More of Flossie's school-life

Our shouts of laughter brought Flossie scampering into the room, evidently in the wildest spirits.

"Horful scandal in 'igh life," she shouted. "A genl'man dish-covered in a lydy's aportments! 'arrowin' details. Speshul! Pyper! Speshul! — Now then, you two, what have you been doing while I've been gone? Suppose you tell me exactly what you've done and I'll tell you exactly what *I've* done!" — then in a tone of cheap melodrama — "Aha! 'ave I surproised yer guilty secret? She winceth! likewise'*e* winceth! in fact they both winceth! Thus h'am I avenged upon the pair!" And kneeling down between us, she pushed a dainty finger softly between the lips of Eva's cunt, and with her other hand took hold of my yard and tenderly frigged it, looking up into our faces all the time with inexpressible love and sweetness shining from her eyes.

"You *dears!*" she said. "It *is* nice to have you two naked together like this!"

A single glance passed between Eva and me, and getting up from our seats we flung ourselves upon the darling and smothered her with kisses. Then Eva, with infinite gentleness and many loving touches, preceded to undress her, handing the dainty garments to me one by one to be laid on the bed near me. As the fair white

93

Flossie: a Venus of fifteen

breasts came forth from the corset, Eva gave a little cry of delight, and pushing the lace-edged chemise below the swelling globes, took one erect and rosy nipple into her mouth, and putting her hand behind my neck, motioned me to take the other. Shivers of delight coursed one another up and down the shapely body over which our fingers roamed in all directions. Flossie's remaining garments were soon allowed to fall by a deft touch from Eva, and the beautiful girl stood before us in all her radiant nakedness. We paused a moment to gaze upon the spectacle of loveliness. The fair face flushed with love and desire; the violet eyes shone; the full rounded breasts put forth their coral nipples as if craving to be kissed again; below the smooth satin belly appeared the silken tuft that shaded without concealing the red lips of the adorable cunt; the polished thighs gained added whiteness by contrast with the dark stockings which clung amorously to the finely moulded legs.

"Now, Jack, *both together*," said Eva, suddenly.

I divined what she meant and arranging a couple of large cushions on the wide divan, I took Flossie in my arms and laid her upon them, her feet upon the floor. Her legs opened in-

More of Flossie's school-life

stinctively and thrusting my head between her thighs, I plunged my tongue into the lower part of the cunt, whilst Eva, kneeling over her, upon the divan, attacked the developed clitoris. Our mouths thus met upon the enchanted spot and our tongues filled every corner and crevice of it. My own, I must admit, occasionally wandered downwards to the adjacent regions, and explored the valley of delight in that direction. But wherever we went and whatever we did, the lithe young body beneath continued to quiver from head to foot with excess of pleasure, shedding its treasures now in Eva's mouth, now in mine and sometimes in both at once! But vivid as were the delights she was experiencing, they were of a passive kind only, and Flossie was already artist enough to know that the keenest enjoyment is only obtained when giving and receiving are equally shared. Accordingly I was not surprised to hear her say:

"Jack, could you come up here to me now, please?"

Signing to me kneel astride of her face, she seized my yard, guided it to her lips and then locking her hands over my loins, she alternately tightened and relaxed her grasp, signifying that I was to use the delicious mouth freely as a substitute for the interdicted opening below. The

Flossie: a Venus of fifteen

peculiar sucking action of her lips, of which I have spoken before, bore a pleasant resemblance to the nipping of an accomplished cunt, whilst the never-resting tongue, against whose soft folds M. Jacques frigged himself luxuriously in his passage between the lips and throat, added a provocation to the lascivious sport not to be enjoyed in the ordinary act of coition. Meanwhile Eva had taken my place between Flossie's legs and was gamahuching the beloved cunt with incredible ardour. A sloping mirror on the wall above enabled me to survey the charming scene at my leisure, and to observe the spasms of delight which, from time to time, shook both the lovely naked forms below me. At last my own time arrived, and Flossie, alert as usual for the signs of approaching crisis, clutched my bottom with convulsive fingers and held me close pressed against her face, whilst I flooded her mouth with the stream of love that she adored. At the same moment the glass told me that Eva's lips were pushing far into the vulva to receive the result of their amorous labours, the passage of which from cunt to mouth was accompanied by every token of intense enjoyment from both the excited girls.

Rest and refreshment were needed by all three after the strain of our morning revels, and

More of Flossie's school-life

so the party broke up for the day after Flossie had mysteriously announced that she was designing something 'extra special', for the morrow.

CHAPTER V

Birthday Festivities

THE NEXT MORNING THERE WAS A NOTE FROM Flossie asking me to come as soon as possible after receiving it.

I hurried to the flat and found Flossie awaiting me, and in one of her most enchanting moods. It was Eva's birthday, as I was now informed for the first time, and to do honour to the occasion, Flossie had put on a costume in which she was to sell flowers at a fancy bazaar a few days later. It consisted of a white Tam-o'-Shanter cap with a straight upstanding feather — a shirt of the thinnest and gauziest white silk falling open at the throat and having a wide sailor collar — a broad lemon-coloured sash, a very short muslin skirt, lemon-coloured silk stockings and high-heeled brown shoes. At the opening of the shirt, a bunch of flame-col-

99

Flossie: a Venus of fifteen

oured roses nestled between the glorious breasts, to the outlines of which all possible prominence was given by the softly clinging material. As she stood waiting to hear my verdict, her red lips slightly parted, a rosy flush upon her cheeks, and love and laughter beaming from the radiant eyes, the magic of her youth and beauty seemed to weave a fresh spell around my heart, and a torrent of passionate words burst from my lips as I strained the lithe young form to my breast and rained kisses upon her hair, her eyes, her cheeks and mouth.

She took my hand in her hand and quietly led me to my favourite chair, and then seating herself on my knee, nestled her face against my cheek and said:

"Oh, Jack, Jack, my darling boy, how can you possibly love me like that!" The sweet voice trembled and a tear or two dropped softly from the violet eyes whilst an arm stole round my neck and the red lips were pressed in a long intoxicating kiss upon my mouth.

We sat thus for some time when Flossie jumped from my knee, and said:

"We are forgetting all about Eva. Come in to her room and see what I have done."

We went hand in hand into the bedroom and

100

Birthday Festivities

found Eva still asleep. On the chairs were laid her dainty garments, to which Flossie silently drew my attention. All along the upper edge of the chemise and corset, round the frills of the drawers and the hem of the petticoat, Flossie had sewn a narrow chain of tiny pink and white rosebuds, as a birthday surprise for her friend. I laughed noiselessly, and kissed her hand in token of my appreciation of the charming fancy.

"Now for Eva's birthday treat," whispered Flossie in my ear. "Go over into that corner and undress yourself as quietly as you can. I will help you."

Flossie's 'help' consisted chiefly in the use of sundry wiles to induce an erection. As these included the slow frigging in which she was such an adept, as well as the application of her rosy mouth and active tongue to every part of my prick, the desired result was rapidly obtained.

"Now, Jack, you are going to have Eva whilst I look on. Some day, my turn will come, and I want to see exactly how to give you the greatest possible amount of pleasure. Come and stand here by me, and we'll wake her up."

We passed round the bed and stood in front of Eva, who still slept on unconscious.

"Ahem!" from Flossie.

101

Flossie: a Venus of fifteen

The sleeping figure turned lazily. The eyes unclosed and fell upon the picture of Flossie in her flower-girl's dress, standing a little behind me and, with her right hand passed in front of me, vigorously frigging my erected yard, whilst the fingers of the other glided with a softly caressing motion over and under the attendant balls.

Eva jumped up, flung off her nightdress and crying to Flossie *"Don't leave go!"* fell on her knees, seized my prick in her mouth and thrust her hand under Flossie's petticoats. The latter, obeying Eva's cry, continued to frig me deliciously from behind, whilst Eva furiously sucked the nut and upper part, and passing her disengaged hand round my bottom, caused me a new and exquisite enjoyment by inserting a dainty finger into the aperture thus brought within her reach. Flossie now drew close up to me and I could feel the swelling breasts in their thin silken covering pressed again my naked back, whilst her hand quickened its maddeningly provoking motion upon my prick and Eva's tongue pursued its enchanted course with increasing ardour and many luscious convolutions. Feeling I was about to spend, Flossie slipped her hand further down towards the root so as to give

102

Birthday Festivities

room for Eva's mouth to engulph almost the whole yard, a hint which the latter was quick to take, for her lips at once pressed close down to Flossie's fingers and with my hands behind my fair gamahucher's neck, I poured my very soul into her waiting and willing throat.

During the interval which followed, I offered my congratulations to Eva and told her how sorry I was not to have known of her birthday before, so that I might have presented a humble gift of some sort. She hastened to assure me that nothing in the world, that I could have brought, would be more welcome than what I had just given her!

Eva had not yet seen her decorated under-clothes and these were now displayed by Flossie with countless merry jokes and quaint remarks. The pretty thought was highly appreciated and nothing would do but our dressing Eva in the flowery garments. When this was done, Flossie suggested a can-can, and the three of us danced a wild *pas-de-trois* until the breath was almost out of our bodies. As we lay panting in various unstudied attitudes of exhaustion, a ring was heard at the door and Flossie, who was the only presentable one of the party went out to answer the summons. She came back in a minute

Flossie: a Venus of fifteen

with an enormous basket of Neapolitan violets. Upon our exclaiming at this extravagance Flossie gravely delivered herself on the following statement.

"Though not in a position for the moment to furnish chapter and verse, I am able to state with conviction that in periods from which we are only separated by some twenty centuries or so, it was customary for ladies and gentlemen of the time to meet and discuss the business of pleasure of the hour without the encumbrance of clothes upon their bodies. The absence of *arrière-pensée* shewn by this commendable practice might lead the superficial to conclude that these discussions led to no practical results. Nothing could be further from the truth. The interviews were invariably held upon a Bank of Violets (so the old writers tell us), and at a certain point in the proceedings, the lady would fall back upon this bank with her legs spread open at the then equivalent to an angle of forty-five. The gentleman would thereupon take in his right (or dexter) hand the instrument which our modern brevity of speech has taught us to call his prick. This, with some trifling assistance on her part, he would introduce into what the same latter-day rage for conciseness of expression

104

Birthday Festivities

leaves us powerless to describe otherwise than as her cunt. On my right we have the modern type of the lady, on my left, that of the gentleman. In the middle, the next best thing to a bank of violets. Ha! you take me at last! Now I'm going to put them all over the bed, and when I'm ready, you, Eva, will kindly oblige by depositing your snowy bottom in the middle, opening your legs and admitting Mr. Jack to the proper position between them."

While delivering this amazing oration, Flossie had gradually stripped herself entirely naked. We both watched her movements in silent admiration as she strewed the bed from end to end with the fragrant blossoms, which filled the room with their delightful perfume. When all was ready, she beckoned to Eva to lay herself on the bed, whispering to her, though not so low but that I could hear.

"Imagine you are Danae. I'll trouble you for the size of Jupiter's prick! Just look at it!" — then much lower, but still audibly — "You're going to be fucked, Eva darling, jolly well fucked! and I'm going to *see* you — *Lovely!*"

The rose-edged chemise and drawers were once more laid aside and the heroine of the day stretched herself voluptuously on the heaped-up

Flossie: a Venus of fifteen

flowers, which sent forth fresh streams of fragrance in response to the pressure of the girl's naked body.

"Ah, a happy thought!" cried Flossie. "If you would lie *across* the bed with your legs hanging down, and Jack wouldn't mind standing up to his work, I think I could be of some assistance to you both."

The change was quickly made, a couple of pillows were slipped under Eva's head, and Flossie, kneeling across the other's face, submitted her cunt to be gamahuched by her friend's tongue which at once darted amorously to its place within the vulva. Flossie returned the salutation for a moment and then resting her chin upon the point just above Eva's clitoris, called to me to "come on". I placed myself in position and was about to storm the breach when Flossie found the near proximity of my yard to be too much for her feelings and begged to be allowed to gamahuche me for a minute.

"After that, I'll be quite good," she added to Eva, "and will only *watch*."

Needless to say I made no objection. The result, as was the case with most of Flossie's actions, was increased pleasure to everybody concerned and to Eva as much as anyone inasmuch

Birthday Festivities

as the divine sucking of Flossie's rosy lips and lust full tongue produced a sensible hardening and lengthening of my excited member.

After performing this delightful service, she was for moving away, but sounds of dissent were heard from Eva, who flung her arms round Flossie's thighs and drew her cunt down in closer contact with the caressing mouth.

From my exalted position, I could see all that was going on and this added enormously to the sensations I began to experience when Flossie, handling my yard with deft fingers, dropped a final kiss upon the nut, and then guided it to the now impatient goal. With eyes lit up with interest and delight, she watched it disappear within the soft red lips whose movements she was near enough to follow closely. Under these conditions, I found myself fucking Eva with unusual vigour and penetration, whilst she, on her part, returned my strokes with powerful thrusts of her bottom and exquisitely pleasurable contractions of her cunt upon my prick.

Flossie, taking in all this with eager eyes, became madly excited, and at last sprang from her kneeling position on the bed, and taking advantage of an *outward* motion of my body, bent down between us, and pushing the point of her

107

Flossie: a Venus of fifteen

tongue under Eva's clitoris, insisted on my finishing the performance with this charming incentive added. Its effect upon both Eva and myself was electric, and as her clitoris and my prick shared equally in the contact of the tongue, we were not long in bringing the entertainment to an eminently satisfactory conclusion.

The next item in the birthday programme was the exhibition of half a dozen cleverly executed pen and ink sketches — Flossie's gift to Eva — shewing the three of us in attitudes not to be found in the illustrations of the "Young Ladies Journal". A discussion arose as to whether Flossie had not been somewhat flattering to the longitudinal dimensions of the present writer's member. She declared that the proportions were "according to *Cocker*" — obviously, as she wittily said, the highest authority on the question.

"Anyhow, I'm going to take measurements and then you'll see I'm right! In the picture the length of Jack's prick is exactly one-third of the distance from his chin to his navel. Now measuring the real article — Hullo! I *say*, Evie, what *have* you done him!"

In point of fact, the object under discussion

Birthday Festivities

was feeling the effects of his recent exercise and had drooped to a partially recumbent attitude.

Eva, who was watching the proceedings with an air of intense amusement called out.

"Take it between your breasts, Flossie; you will see a difference then!"

The mere prospect of such a lodging imparted a certain amount of vigour to Monsieur Jacques, who was thereupon introduced into the delicious cleft of Flossie's adorable bosom, and in rapture at the touch of the soft flesh on either side of him, at once began to assume more satisfactory proportions.

"But he's not up to his full height yet," said Flossie. "Come and help me, Evie dear; stand behind Jack and frig him whilst I gamahuche him in front. *That's* the way to get him up to concert pitch! When I feel him long and stiff enough in my mouth, I'll get up and take his measure."

The success of Flossie's plan was immediate and complete, and when the measurements were made, the proportions were found to be exactly twenty-one and seven inches respectively, whilst in the drawing they were three inches to one inch. Flossie proceeded to execute a wild war-

109

Flossie: a Venus of fifteen

dance of triumph over this signal vindication of her accuracy, winding up by insisting on my carrying her pick-a-back round the flat. Her enjoyment of this ride was unbounded, as also was mine, for besides the pleasure arising from the close contact of her charming body, she contrived to administer a delicious friction to my member with the calves of her naked legs.

On our return to the bedroom, Eva was sitting on the edge of the low divan.

"Bring her to me here," she cried.

I easily divined what was wanted, and carrying my precious burden across the room, I faced round with my back to Eva. In the sloping glass to the left, I could see her face disappear between the white rounded buttocks, at the same moment that her right moved in front of me and grasped my yard which it frigged with incomparable tenderness and skill. This operation was eagerly watched by Flossie over my shoulder, while she clung to me with arms and legs and rubbed herself against my loins with soft undulating motions like an amorous kitten, the parting lips of her cunt kissing my back and her every action testifying to the delight with which she was receiving the attentions of Eva's tongue upon the neighbouring spot.

110

Birthday Festivities

My feelings were now rapidly passing beyond my control, and I had to implore Eva to remove her hand, whereupon Flossie, realising the state of affairs, jumped down from her perch, and burying my prick in her sweet mouth, sucked and frigged me in such a frenzy of desire that she had very soon drawn from me the last drop I had to give her.

A short period of calm ensued after this last ebullition, but Flossie was in too mad a mood to-day to remain long quiescent.

"Eva" she suddenly cried, "I believe I am as tall as you nowadays, and I am *quite sure* my breasts are as large as yours. I'm going to measure and see!"

After Eva's height had been found to be only a short inch above Flossie's, the latter proceeded to take the most careful and scientific measurements of the breasts. First came the circumference, then the diameter *over* the nipples, then the diameter omitting the nipples, then the distance from the nipple to the upper and lower edges of the hemispheres, and so on. No dryasdust old savant, staking his reputation upon an absolutely accurate calculation of the earth's surface, could have carried out his task with more ineffable solemnity than did this

Flossie: a Venus of fifteen

merry child who, one knew, was all the time secretly bubbling over with the fun of her quaint conceit.

The result was admitted to be what Flossie called it — "a moral victory" for herself, inasmuch as half a square inch, or as Flossie declared, "fifteen thirty-*two-ths*", was all the superiority of area that Eva could boast.

"There's one other measurement I *should* like to have taken," said Eva, "because in spite of my ten years '*de plus*' and the fact that my cunt is not altogether a stranger to the joys of being fucked, I believe that Flossie would win *that* race, and I should like her to have one out of three!"

"*Lovely!*" cried Flossie. "But Jack must be the judge. Here's the tape, Jack: fire away. Now, Evie, come and lie beside me on the edge of the bed, open your legs, and swear to abide by the verdict!"

After a few minutes fumbling with the tape and close inspection of the parts in dispute, I retired to a table and wrote down the following, which I pinned against the window-curtain.

112

Birthday Festivities

Letchford v. Eversley.

Mesdames,

In compliance with your instructions I have this day surveyed the private premises belonging to the above parties, and have now the honour to submit the following report, plan, and measurements.

As will be seen from the plan, Miss Letchford's cunt is exactly 3 1/16 inches from the underside of clitoris to the base of vulva. Miss Eversley's cunt, adopting the same line of measurement, gives 3 5/8 inches.

I may add that the premises appear to me to be thoroughly desirable in both cases, and to a good, upright and painstaking tenant would afford equally pleasant accommodation in spring, summer, autumn or winter.

A small but well-wooded covert is attached to each, whilst an admirable dairy is in convenient proximity.

With reference to the Eversley property, I am informed that it has not yet been occupied, but in view of its size and beauty, and the undoubted charms of the surrounding country, I confidently anticipated that a permanent and satisfactory tenant (such as I have ventured to describe above), will very shortly be found for it. My opinion of its advantages as a place of resi-

113

Flossie: a Venus of fifteen

dence may, indeed, be gathered from the fact that I am greatly disposed to make an offer in my own person.

Yours faithfully,
J. Archer,

As the two girls stood with their hands behind their backs reading my ultimatum, Flossie laughed uproariously, but I noticed that Eva looked grave and thoughtful.

Had I written anything that annoyed her? I could hardly think so, but while I was meditating on the possibility, half resolved to put it to the test by a simple question, Eva took Flossie and myself by the hand, led us to the sofa and sitting down between us, said:

"Listen to me, you two dears! You, Flossie, are my chosen darling, and most beloved little friend. You Jack, are Flossie's lover, and for her sake as well as for your own, I have the greatest affection for you. You both know all this. Well, I have not the heart to keep you from one another any longer. Flossie, dear, I hereby absolve you from your promise to me. Jack, you have behaved like a brick, as you are. Come here to-morrow at your usual time and I think we shall be able to agree upon '*a tenant for the Eversley property.*'"

Birthday Festivities

This is not a novel of sentiment, and a description of what followed would therefore be out of place. Enough to say that after one wild irrepressible shriek of joy and gratitude from Flossie, the conversation took a sober and serious turn, and soon afterwards we parted for the day.

CHAPTER VI

The tenant in possession

THE NEXT MORNING'S POST BROUGHT ME LET-
ters from both, Eva and Flossie.

"My dear Jack (wrote the former),

"Tomorrow will be a red-letter day for you
two! and I want you both to get the utmost of
delight from it. So let no sort of scruple or com-
punction spoil your pleasure. Flossie is, in
point of physical development, a woman. As
such, she longs to be fucked by the man she
loves. Fuck her therefore with all and more
than all the same skill and determination you
displayed in fucking me. She can think and
talk of nothing else. Come early to-morrow and
bring your admirable prick in its highest state
of efficiency and stiffness!

"Yours
"Eva".

Flossie: a Venus of fifteen

Flossie wrote:

"I cannot sleep a wink for thinking of what is coming to me to-morrow. All the time I keep turning over in my mind how best to make it nice for you. I am practising Eva's 'nip.' I *feel* as if I could do it, but nipping *nothing* is not really practice, is it, Jack? My beloved, I kiss your prick, in imagination. To-morrow I will do it in the flesh, for I warn you that nothing will ever induce me to give up *that*, nor will even the seven inches which I yearn to have in my cunt ever bring me to consent to being depried of the sensation of your dear tongue when it curls between the lips and pays polite attentions to my clitoris! But you shall have me as you like to-morrow, and all days to follow. I am to be in the future.

> "Yours body and soul
> "Flossie."

When I arrived at the flat I found Flossie had put on the costume in which I had seen her the first day of our acquaintance. The lovely little face wore an expression of gravity, as though to shew me she was not forgeting the importance of the occasion. I am not above confessing that, for my part, I was profoundly moved.

The tenant in possession

We sat beside one another, hardly exchanging a word. Presently Flossie said.

"Whenever you are *ready*, Jack, I'll go to my room and undress."

The characteristic "naiveté of this remark somewhat broke the spell that was upon us, and I kissed her with effusion.

"Shall it be . . . *quite* naked, Jack?"

"Yes, darling, if *you* don't mind."

"All right. When I am ready I'll call to you."

Five minutes later, I heard the welcome summons.

From the moment I found myself in her room, all sense of restraint vanished at a breath. She flew at me in a perfect fury of desire, pushed me by sheer force upon my back on the bed, and lying at full length upon me with her face close to mine, she said.

"Because I was a girl and not a woman, Jack, you have never fucked me. But you are going to fuck me now, and I shall be a woman. But first, I want to be a girl to you still for a few minutes only. I want to have your dear prick in my mouth again; I want you to kiss my cunt in the old delicious way; I want to lock my naked arms round your naked body; and hold you to my face, whilst I wind my tongue round your prick until you spend. Let me do all this,

119

Flossie: a Venus of fifteen

Jack, and then you shall fuck me till the skies fall."

Without giving me time to reply to this frenzied little oration, Flossie had whisked round and was in position for the double gamahuche she desired. Parting her legs to their widest extent on each side of my face, she sank gently down until her cunt came full upon my open mouth. At the same moment I felt my prick seized and plunged deep into her mouth with which she at once commenced the delicious sucking action I knew so well. I responded by driving my tongue to the root into the rosy depths of her perfumed cunt, which I sucked with ever increasing zest and enjoyment, drawing fresh treasures from its inner recesses at every third or fourth stroke of my tongue. Words fail me to describe the unparalleled vigour of her sustained attack upon my erected prick, which she sucked, licked, tongued and frigged with such a furious *abandon* and at the same time with such a subtle skill and knowledge of the sublime art of gamahuching, that the end came with unusual rapidity, and wave after wave of the sea of love broke in ecstasy upon the 'coral strand' of her adorable mouth. For a minute or two more, her lips retained their hold and then, leaving her position, she came and lay down be-

120

The tenant in possession

side me, nestling her naked body against mine, and softly chafing the lower portion of my prick whilst she said:

"Now, Jack darling, I am going to talk to you about the different ways of fucking, because of course you will want to fuck me, and I shall want to be fucked, in every possible position, and in every single part of my body where a respectable young woman may reasonable *ask* to be fucked.

The conversation which followed agreeably filled the intervening time before the delicate touches which Flossie kept constantly applying to my prick caused it to raise its head to a considerable altitude, exhibiting a hardness and rigidity which gave high promise for the success of the coming encounter.

"Good Gracious!" cried Flossie, "do you think I shall ever find room for all that, Jack?"

"For that, and more also, sweetheart," I replied.

"*More!* Why *what* more are you going to put into me?"

"This is the only article I propose to introduce at present, Floss. But I mean that when Monsieur Jacques finds himself for the first time with his head buried between the delicious cushions in *there*" (*touching her belly*) "he

121

Flossie: a Venus of fifteen

will most likely beat his own record in the matter ter of length and stiffness."

"Do you mean, Jack, that he will be bigger with me than he was with Eva?" said Flossie with a merry twinkle.

"Certainly I mean it," was my reply. "To fuck a beautiful girl like Eva must always be immensely enjoyable, but to fuck a young Venus of fifteen, who besides being the perfection of mortal loveliness, is also one's own chosen and adorable little sweetheart — *that* belongs to a different order of pleasure altogether.

"And I suppose, Jack, that when the fifteen-year-old is simply dying to be fucked by her lover, as I am at this moment, the chances are that she may be able to make it rather nice for him, as well as absolutely heavenly for herself. Now I can wait no longer. 'First position' at once, please, Jack. Give me your prick in my hand and I will direct his wandering footsteps."

"He's at the door, Flossie; shall he enter?"

"Yes. Push him in slowly and fuck gently at first, so that I may find out by degrees how much he's going to hurt me. A little further, Jack. Why, he's more than half way in already! Now you keep still and I'll thrust a little with my bottom."

The tenant in possession

"Why, Floss, you darling, you're nipping me deliciously!"

"Can you feel me Jack? How lovely! Fuck me a little more, Jack, and get in deeper, that's it! Now faster and harder. What glorious pleasure it is!"

"And no pain, darling?"

"Not a scrap. One more good push and he'll be in up to the hilt, won't he? Eva told me to put my legs over your back. Is that right?"

"Quite right, and if you're sure I'm not hurting you, Floss, I'll really begin now and fuck you in earnest."

"That's what I'm here for, Sir," she replied with a touch of her never absent fun even in this supreme moment.

"Here goes, then!" I answered. Having once made up her mind that she had nothing to dread, Flossie abandoned herself with enthusiasm to the pleasures of the moment. Locking her arms round my neck and her legs round my buttocks, she cried to me to fuck her with all my might.

"Drive your prick into me again and again, Jack. Let me feel your belly against mine. Did you feel my cunt nip you then? Ah! how you are fucking me now! — fucking me, fu . . . u . . . ucking me!"

Her lovely eyes turned to heaven, her breath

123

Flossie: a Venus of fifteen

came in quick short gasps, her fingers wandered feverishly about my body. At last, with a cry, she plunged her tongue into my mouth and, with convulsive undulations of the little body, let loose the floods of her being to join the deluge which, with sensations of exquisite delight, I poured into her burning cunt.

The wild joy of this our first act of coition was followed by a slight reaction and, with a deep sigh of contentment Flossie fell asleep in my arms, leaving my prick still buried in its natural resting-place. Before long, my own eyelids closed and, for an hour or more, we lay thus gaining from blessed sleep fresh strength to enter upon new transports of pleasure.

Flossie was the first to awake, stirred no doubt by the unaccustomed sensations of a swelling prick within her. I awoke to find her dear eyes resting upon my face, her naked arms round my neck and her cunt enfolding my yard with a soft and clinging embrace.

Her bottom heaved gently, and accepting the invitation thus tacitly given, I turned my little sweetheart on her back and, lying luxuriously between her widely parted legs, once more drove my prick deep into her cunt and fucked her with slow lingering strokes, directed upwards so as to

124

The tenant in possession

bring all possible contact to bear upon the clitoris.

This particular motion afforded her evident delight and the answering thrusts of her bottom were delivered with ever increasing vigour and precision, each of us relishing to the full the efforts of the other to augment the pleasure of the encounter. With sighs and gasps and little cries of rapture, Flossie strained me to her naked breasts, and twisting her legs tightly round my own, cried out that she was spending and implored me to let her feel my emission mix with hers. By dint of clutching her bottom with my hands, driving the whole length of my tongue into her mouth I was just able to manage the simultaneous discharge she coveted, and once more I lay upon her in a speechless ecstasy of consummated passion.

Any one of my readers who has had the supreme good fortune to fuck the girl of his heart will bear me out in saying that the lassitude following upon such a meeting is greater and more lasting than the mere weariness resulting from an ordinary act of copulation 'where love is not'.

Being well aware of this fact, I resolved that my beloved little Flossie's powers should not be taxed any further for the moment, and told her so.

125

Flossie: a Venus of fifteen

"But Jack," she cried, almost in tears, "we've only done it *one* way, and Eva says there are at least *six*! And oh, I do *love* it so!"

"And so do I, little darling. But also, I love *you*, and I'm not going to begin by giving you and that delicious little caressing cunt of yours more work than is good for you both."

"Oh, dear! I suppose you're right, Jack."

"Of course I'm right, darling. To-morrow I shall come and fuck you again, and the next day, and the next, and many days after that. It will be odd if we don't find ourselves in Eva's six different positions before we've done!"

At this moment Eva herself entered the room.

"Well, Flossie . . . ?" she said.

"Ask Jack!" replied Flossie.

"Well Jack, then . . . ?" said Eva.

"Ask Flossie!" I retorted, and fled from the room.

The adventures I have, with many conscious imperfections, related in the foregoing pages, were full of interest to me, and were, I am disposed to think, not without their moments of attraction for my fellow-actors in the scenes depicted.

It by no means necessarily follows that they will produce a corresponding effect upon the reading public who, in my descriptions of Flossie

126

The tenant in possession

and her ways, may find only an ineffectual attempt to set forth the charms of what appears to me an absolutely unique temperament. If haply it should prove to be otherwise, I should be glad to have the opportunity of continuing a veritable labour of love by recounting certain further experiences of Eva, Flossie and

Yours faithfully
"Jack."

Eveline

CHAPTER 1

"A temperament like yours, my darling child, requires constant attention. You are no ordinary girl. You have need of change, of variety, of sufficient venereal food to keep you in health. You have developed within you so much vitality, so much necessity for sensual gratification—if I may use the term—that you have urgent need to feed the fire. Like the ancient flame that burned, which still burns, on the altars of the followers of Zoroaster, you must keep it going, replenishing it as may be necessary, never letting it languish. If it does so you will not be well. Eveline will not be herself."

"I feel the force of what you say, dear Papa. I love you devotedly . . . but . . ."

"Yes, my child, I see it, I know it. At my age, with all my various engagements and occupations, I am not likely to be all to you that your nature demands. When you are married . . ."

"Do not speak of that, dear. It will be time enough hereafter. I do not anticipate any pleasure from my married state—not in the sense that my dear Papa can bestow it. I look forward to it with disgust, rather than with satisfaction. And I feel very dejected on the subject."

"Listen to me, Eveline. Your nature requires sexual excitement. You know it as well as I do. It is medicine to you. You must take your medicine or be unhealthy. Take it then, only be careful that you imbibe naught but what is good and wholesome. I would be your doctor if you would follow my advice."

"I am always ready to be guided by your counsel, dear Papa."

"Well then, Eveline, having sufficiently explained my views, which I am sure you understand, I will obtain for you the best medicine."

"And I will take it, for whatever you provide for little Eveline is sure to be nice."

"It shall be something extra nice. Something that will set your pretty mouth watering, your eyes sparkling, your whole being alert with anticipation of enjoyment. Something that will ring sobs of delight from your darling heart, sighs of the most intense rapture from your parted lips, something which shall possess your body and your senses with ecstasy, something irresistible in its noble manhood—solid, stiff, strong!"

"Oh Papa, you excite me too much! I already long for this delicious medicine. When may I commence my course of it? Or is it only in small doses, to be taken sparingly? I am ready for all. Let it be large and solid—stiff and strong!"

"Your capacity for enjoyment is wonderful, my child. You require a male well-furnished with sexual organs in full vigor, robust and extraordinarily well-developed. I will provide you with such. I will enable you to take your fill of pleasure without risk, without danger."

"I think you are right, Papa. In the meantime I want this thing which is always stiff in my hand. See how the head shines! It enters! Oh goodness, dear! How you excite your little girl! Push now! Oh, it comes! It is squirting into me—Oh! Give me all your delicious seed. Dear love! You kill me with pleasure."

"I have in store for you, my darling child, a delicious treat for the senses. To see you enjoy it will be to me also an extreme pleasure. We will roll in ecstasy. Our senses shall float in a world of pleasure. Give me only a few days to arrange it. Your medicine will take a novel form. The medium is deaf and dumb."

"Oh, Papa, how dreadful!"

"By no means, Eveline, we only desire the means, the instrument. So long as that has no surroundings which are positively objectionable or repulsive, it matters little; we shall possess all we require. I promise you that in the present case, it is neither, but on the other hand, attractive in every sense. You will be charmed and even sympathetic when you know more."

"You excite my curiosity, Papa. When may I take the first dose?"

"As soon as we are back in town together. They say the implement of love is immense and that its owner is singularly gifted in sexual gratifications."

"Oh, Papa, you are too good to your naughty little Eveline. You offer her a banquet—it will not be medicine. It will be a draught of pleasure. My mouth waters already. I long to taste it."

*　*　*

Percy had been at Eastbourne three days. We had not altogether lost our time. I determined to run up to town. I went by an early train, alone. I entered the station some 15 minutes before the train started. On the platform was a gentlemanly-looking man in a tweed suit. I thought I had seen his face before. We passed each other. He looked pointedly at me. Certainly I knew his features. I never forget, if I take an interest in a man's appearance. I liked the looks of this tall, well-built fellow in tweed. He appeared to be about 35 or 40 years of age, hale and hearty. I gave him one of my glances as he passed me.

"This way, Miss. First-class. No corridors on this train. You will be all right here. You're all alone at present."

"Thank you, guard. Does the train go without stopping?"

"Stops at Lewes, Miss. That's all—then right up."

I saw my tall friend pass the carriage. Another glance. He stopped, hesitated, then opened the door and got in. He took a seat

14

opposite me. The newspaper appeared to engross his attention until the whistle sounded.

"Would you mind if I were to lower the window? These carriages are stuffy. The morning is so warm."

I made no objection, but smilingly gave my consent.

"How calm and beautiful the sea looks. It seems a pity to leave it."

"Indeed I think so—especially for London."

"You are going to London? How odd! So am I."

I could not be mistaken. I had seen him somewhere before.

"I shall miss the sea very much. We have no sea baths in Manchester. I love my morning dip."

It struck me like a flash. I remembered him now.

"You must have enjoyed it very much, coming from an inland city."

"Well, yes, you see I had a good time. They looked after me well. Always had my machine ready."

"I have no doubt of that."

"Number 33. A new one—capital people—very fine machine."

I suppose I smiled a little. He laughed in reply as he read my thoughts. Then he folded up his paper. I arranged my small reticule. It unfortunately dropped from my hand. He picked it up and presented it to me. His foot touched mine. We conversed. He told me he lived near Manchester. He had been to Eastbourne for a rest. His business had been too much for him, but he was all right now. His

.15

gaze was constantly on me. I kept thinking about his appearance all naked on the platform of the bathing machine as old David Jones rowed me past. We stopped at Lewes.

My companion put his head out of the window. He prevented the entry of an old lady by abusing the newspaper boy for his want of activity.

"I think Eastbourne is one of the best bathing places on the coast. You know, where the gentlemen's machines are!"

"I think I know where they keep them."

"Well, I was going to say . . . but . . . well . . . what a funny girl you are! Why are you laughing?"

"Because I was thinking of a funny idea. I was thinking of a friend."

His foot pushed a little closer. Very perceptible was the touch. He never ceased gloating over my person. My gloves evidently had an especial attraction for him. Meanwhile I looked him well over. He was certainly a fine man. He aroused my emotions. I permitted his foot to remain in contact with mine. I even moved it past his so that our ankles touched. His face worked nervously. Poor man, no wonder! He gave me a seaching look. Our glances met. He pressed my leg between his own. His fingers were trembling with that undefined longing for contact with the object of desire I so well understood. I smiled.

"You seem very fond of the ladies."

I said it boldly, with a familiar meaning. He could not fail to understand. I glanced at his leather bag in the rack above.

"I cannot deny the soft impeachment. I am.

16

Especially when they are young and beautiful."

"Oh, you men. You are dreadfully wicked. What would Mrs. Turner say to that?"

I laughed. He stared with evident alarm. It was a bold stroke. I risked it. Either way I lost nothing.

"How do you know I'm married?"

My shaft had gone home. He had actually missed the first evident fact. He picked it up, however, quickly, before I could reply.

"It appears you know me, you know my name."

"Well, yes, you see I'm not blind."

It was his turn to laugh.

"Ah, you had me there. What a terribly observant woman you are."

He seized my hand before I could regain my attitude. He pressed it with both of his.

"You will not like me any the less, will you?"

"On the contrary, they say married men are the best."

Up to this point my effrontery had led him on. He must have felt that he was on safe ground. My last remark was hardly even equivocal. He evidently took it as it was intended. I was actually excited. The man and the opportunity tempted me. I wanted him. I was delighted with his embarrassment, with his first and fast increasing assurance. He crossed over. He occupied the seat beside me. My gloved hand remained in his.

"I am so glad you think so. You do not know how charming I think you. Married men ought to be good judges, you know."

"I suppose so. I rather prefer them."

17

He looked into my face and I laughed as I uttered the words. He brought his face very close. He pressed his left hand around my waist. I made no resistance. The carriage gave a sympathetic jerk as it rushed along. Our faces touched. His lips were in contact with mine. It was quite accidental, of course; the line is so badly laid. We kissed.

"Oh, you are nice! How pretty you are!"

He pressed his hot lips again to mine. I thought of the sight I had seen on the bathing machine. My blood boiled. I half-closed my eyes. I let him keep his lips on mine. He pressed me to him. He drew my light form to his stout and well-built body as in a vise. I put my right foot up on the opposite seat. He stared at the pretty, tight little kid boot. He was evidently much agitated.

"Ah, what a lovely boot!"

He touched it with his hand. His fingers ran over the soft cream-colored leather. I wore a pair of Papa's prime favorites. He did not stop there. The trembling hand passed on to my stockings, advancing by stealthy degrees. It was then he tried to push forward the tip of his tongue.

"How beautiful you are and how gentle and kind!"

His arm enfolded me still closer; my bosom pressed his shoulder. His hand advanced further and further up my stocking. I closed my knees resolutely. I gave a hurried glance around.

"Are we quite safe here, do you think?"

"Quite safe and as you see, alone."

Our lips met again. This time I kissed him

18

boldly. The tip of his active tongue inserted itself between my moist lips.

"Ah how lovely you are! How gloriously pretty!"

"Hush! They might hear us in the next carriage. I am frightened."

"You are deliciously sweet. I long for you dreadfully."

Mr. Turner's hand continued its efforts to reach my knees. I relaxed my pressure a little. He reached my garters above them. In doing so he uncovered my ankles. He feasted his eyes on my calves daintily set off in open-work stockings of a delicate shade.

It was a delicious game of seduction. I enjoyed his lecherous touches. He was constantly becoming more confident in his sudden and uncontrollable passion. He strained me to him. His breath came quick and sweet on my face. I lusted for this man's embrace beyond all power of language to convey. His warm hand reached my plump thigh. I made a pretense to prevent his advance.

"Pray, Oh pray, do not do that! Oh!"

A sudden jerk as we apparently sped over some joints. I relaxed my resistance a little. He took instant advantage of the movement. His finger was on the most sensitive of my private parts. It pressed upon my clitoris. I felt the little thing stiffen, swell and throb under the touch of a man's hand. His excitement increased. He drew me ever closer. He pressed my warm body to his. His kisses, hot and voluptuous, covered my neck and face.

"How divinely sweet you are! The perfume

of your lovely breath is so rapturously nice. Do let me—do—do! I love you."

He held me tight with his left arm. He had withdrawn his right. I was conscious he was undoing his trousers. He had left my skirts in disorder. I saw him pull aside his protruding shirt. I secretly watched his movements out of a corner of my eye while he kept my face close to him. Then appeared all that I had seen in the bathing machine. But standing erect. Red-headed and formidable. A huge limb. He thrust it into full view.

"My darling! My beauty! See this! To what a savage state you have driven me! You will let me, won't you?"

"Oh, for shame, let me go! Pray do not do that! You must not! Your finger hurts. Don't!"

The jolting of the carriage favored his operations. His hand was again between my legs. His second finger pressed my button. His parts were bedewed with the fluid begotten by desire. He was inspecting the premises before taking possession. I only hoped he would not find the accommodation insufficient.

"Oh, pray, don't! Oh, goodness! What a man you are!"

With a sudden movement he slipped around upon his knees, passing one of my legs over his left arm and thus thrust me back on the soft spring seat of the carriage. He threw up my clothes. He was between my thighs. My belly and private parts were exposed to his lascivious operations. I looked over my dress as I attempted to right myself. I saw him kneeling before me in the most indelicate position. His trousers were open. He had loosened

20

his clothing so much that his testicles were out. I saw all in that quick feverish glance. His belly was covered with crisp hair. I saw the dull red head of his big limb drawn downward by the little string as it faced my way, and the slitlike opening from which the men spurt their white sap.

He audaciously took my hand, gloved as it was, and placed it upon his member. It was hard and rigid as wood.

"Feel that—dear girl! Do not be frightened. I will not hurt you. Feel, feel my prick!"

He drew me forward. I felt him as requested. I had ceased all resistance. My willing little hand clasped the immense instrument he called his "prick."

"Now put it there yourself, little girl. It is longing to be into you."

"Oh, my good heavens! It will never go in. You will kill me!"

Nevertheless I assisted him to his enjoyment. I put the nut between the nether lips. He pushed while firmly holding me by both hips. My parts relaxed. My vagina adapted itself as I had been told it could without injury to the most formidable of male organs. The huge thing entered me. He thrust in fierce earnest. He got fairly in.

"Oh, my God! I'm into you now! Oh, how delicious! Hold tight. Let me pull you down to me! Oh, how soft!"

I passed my left arm through the strap. My right clutched him round the neck. He pulled down his hand. He parted the strained lips around his intruding weapon. Then he seized

21

me by the buttocks. He strained me towards him as he pushed. My head fell back—my lips parted. I felt his testicles rubbing close up between my legs. He was into me to the quick.

"Oh, dear, you are too rough. My goodness me! How you are tearing me! Oh! Oh! Ah, it is too much! You darling man. Push—Push—Oh!"

It was too much pleasure. I threw my head back again. I grasped the cushions on either side. I could only gasp and moan now. I moved my head from side to side as he lay down on my belly and enjoyed me. His thing —stiff as a staff—worked up and down in my vagina. I could feel the big plumlike gland pushed forcibly against my womb. I spent over and over again. I was in heaven.

He ground his teeth. He hissed. He lolled his head. He kissed me on the lips, breathing hard and fast. His pleasure was delicious to witness.

"Oh, hold tight, love! I am in an agony of pleasure! I . . . I can't tell you! I never tasted such delicious poking! Oh!"

"Oh dear! Oh dear! You are so large . . . so strong!"

"Don't move! Don't pinch my prick more than you can help, darling girl. Let us go on as long as possible. You are coming again, I can feel you squeezing me. Oh, wait a moment! So! Hold still!"

"Oh, I can feel it at my waist! Oh! Oh You are so stiff"

"I cannot hold much longer, I must spend soon!"

Bang! Bang! Bang!

The train was passing over the joints at Reigate. The alarm was sufficient to retard our climax. It acted as a check to his wild excitement; it was too much pleasure. I threw my head back again. I grasped the cushions on either side. I could not speak. I could not gasp again as before.

"Hold quite still, you sweet little beauty! We do not stop, the seed is quickening up again. Now push! Is that nice? Do you like my big prick? Does it stir you up? You are right, my sweet, I can feel your little womb to the tip."

He assisted me to throw my legs over his shoulders. He seemed to enter me further than ever.

"Oh, you are so large! Oh, good Lord! Go on slowly—don't finish yet. It's so . . . so . . . nice! You're making me come again. Oh!"

"No, dear, I won't finish you before I can help it. You are so nice to poke slowly. Do you like being finished? Do you like to feel a man come?"

"Oh, not so hard! There . . . oh, my! Must I tell you? I . . . I . . . love to feel . . . to feel a man spend . . . all the sweet sperm."

"You'll feel mine very soon. Very soon, you beautiful little angel. Oh! I shall swim in it. There. My prick is in up to the balls! Oh! How you nip it!"

He gave me some exquisite short stabs with his loins. His thing, as hard as wood, was up in my belly as far as it would go. He sank his head on my shoulder.

23

"Hold still . . . I'm spending! Oh, my God!"

I felt a little gush from him. It flowed in quick jets as he groaned in his ecstasy. I opened my legs and raised my loins to receive it. I clutched right and left at anything and everything. I spent furiously. He gave me a quantity. I was swimming in it. At length he desisted and released me.

A few minutes sufficed in which to arrange ourselves decently. Mr. Turner asked me many questions. I fenced some—I answered others. I led him to believe I was professionally employed in a provincial company. I told him I had been ill and had been resting a short time in Eastbourne. He was delicate enough not to press me for particulars. But he asked for an address. I gave him a country post office. In a few minutes more we stopped on the river bridge to deliver our tickets.

The train rolled into the station. My new friend made his exit. He dexterously slipped two sovereigns into my glove as he squeezed my hand. I was glad. It proved the complete success of my precautions.

I hailed a hansom and drove direct to Swan and Edgars. Outside the station my cab stopped in a crowd. A poor woman thrust a skinny arm and hand towards me with an offer of a box of matches. I took them and substituted one of the sovereigns. As I alighted in Picadilly a ragged little urchin made a dash to turn back the door of my cab. He looked half-starved.

"Have you a mother? How many brothers and sisters?"

"Six of us, lady. Muvver's out of work."

"Take that home as quick as you can!"

He took the other sovereign and dashed off. He had never been taught to say thank you. I discharged the cab. I made sure I was not followed.

* * *

I drove home. I found Mrs. Lockett ready to receive me. It was yet morning. I lunched alone. John was radiant with happiness.

"No more chicken, thank you, John. How is Robin? There are some ginger nuts for him in a bag on the hall table. You see I did not forget him."

"Thank you very much, Miss. It's been dull every since you went away. Mrs. Lockett ain't very lively company. As for Robin, Miss, he's been sulky as possible; the poor thing is quite alone. In the morning he comes up to the bed clothes and stares me in the face, Miss, as much to say 'where've you gone to?' I'm ashamed to look at him."

"Poor dear. Why, John, how shocking! It's quite stiff now."

I had only just tapped it with my fingertips through the red plush breeches. The unruly monster was already stretching itself down his plump thigh as its owner leaned forward to pour me a glass of wine. The door was shut. I let fly a button.

"Oh, John, it's shameful! It's bigger than ever!"

I gave a twist of the wrist. His fat member sprang out into view. I squeezed it as I ex-

25

amined the rubicund top. What a beauty it was! The true perfection of what such things ought to be. I pulled down the skin. I delighted to see the effect of my touches.

"He likes that, John, doesn't he? He seems to enjoy being stroked like a cat."

"Yes, Miss—puts up his back for it. You can almost hear him purr."

"You must not let him get too much excited. We will keep all that for tonight, John. I think we must let him out then. But you cannot be too cautious. Mrs. Lockett sleeps in the wing, doesn't she?"

"Yes, Miss. She always turns the key of the door on the landing when she locks it at night. The maid sleeps on the top floor. There is no one on your floor now, Miss."

I made my arrangements. I finished my lunch, then dressed myself very plainly to go out. John called a cab. I drove straight to my bootmaker in Great Castle Street. Monsieur Dalmaine was not an ordinary bootmaker. He was an artist in boots. He made only for ladies, and his terms would be considered extravagant by the ordinary customer. His shop was small and unpretentious. Personally, he was short and stout, and fair for a Frenchman. He might have been some eight and thirty. His wife kept the accounts and assisted him to collect them. His boots and shoes were not ordinary, either. They were the perfection of his craft. He took real pride in them. The ability of the poor man to turn out boots to my satisfaction, and what seemed of greater importance, to his own, was sufficient. He was in the shop when I entered. Madame

Dalmaine was out collecting accounts as usual on a Monday afternoon.

"Good morning, Mr. Dalmaine. Are my boots *couleur creme*, ready? Have you completed the slight alterations to the pale blue lace boots?"

"Both are at your service, Miss. I will try them on if you will step into the showroom."

There was a small, well-arranged room behind the shop with several large glass cases. In these were deposited boots that had been made for celebrities. They were by no means old or worn, but this most extraordinary man had obtained them from the ladies in question after they had only served a single occasion. Monsieur Dalmaine claimed that they did not please him. He thereupon supplied a second pair. He obtained the first for his *musée*, as he called it.

I sat myself in an easy chair in which he fitted all his lady customers. It was a great event if he made a pair of boots in a fortnight. He had, however, prepared mine considerably within that period. He brought out both pairs. He held them up. He turned them about. His keen little gray eyes sparkled with evident pleasure.

"*Les voila*, Mademoiselle! But they are superb. It is not often that I make for so beautiful a foot. *Mon Dieu!* One would say the foot of Mademoiselle had been sculptured by Canova himself. It is a study."

He knelt before me. He placed my foot, in its openwork silk stocking, upon his knee. He gave one affectionate look at the object. He cast another at his work. He then proceeded

27

to fit the artistic little boot. Several times he inserted my foot. As often he withdrew it to make some trifling adjustment. I tired of his minuteness. I amused myself in worrying the good man by avoiding his grasps. Sometimes I slipped my glossy little silk-covered foot on one side, sometimes on the other. At last it slid from the approaching boot and was jerked between his thighs. There it alighted on the muscular development of Monsieur Dalmaine's most private personal effects. I distinctly felt something pulsate between my toes. The artist of ladies' boots flushed. He was arranging the lace of the new *chaussure*.

"Please give it to me, Monsieur Dalmaine. I have not yet examined it for myself. Is not the toe more pointed than usual? You know I do not wear those hideously impossible toes to my boots."

He handed it up, holding my ankle as he did so. I rubbed my wicked foot a little more gently against his person as I took the boot from his hand. At the same time the man must have seen the half-comical, half-lecherous glance with which I met his eyes. A sudden inspiration almost overwhelmed me. This artist *cordonnier* was a victim of his own creations.

He had fallen in love with his own work like Pygmalion with his statue. The discovery set me on fire at once. What joy to play on this man's weakness. I allowed him to fit on the boot. He smoothed down the yielding kid as it glistened with its soft sheen on my foot. His eyes followed his nervous fingers. His lips moved as though he longed, yet dared not ex-

28

tend his too evident fascination into actual embrace. I then pushed my toe again towards his person. The quick blood of the nervous Frenchman was plainly stirred. There was an unmistakable enlargement in the region of his trouble. My warm foot did not let it subside. I was conscious of a certain throbbing on the sole of my foot.

"How long have you been in business, Monsieur Dalmaine? You evidently have a passion for your work. You are not like the ordinary bootmaker."

"No, Mademoiselle, I am not so. I am a man different. I am one man by myself. No other man understands me. Sometimes a lady comes to see me. I fit them to her. I make the boots for her. She likes my work—she comes again. More work, more boots. But— oh no! she comprehends not. She knows not my heart!"

Monsieur Dalmaine pressed his hand over the part mentioned. He bowed his head with its light curly hair over my legs as he knelt in the pursuit of his calling. His air was impatient, if not content to suffer.

"What is the matter with your heart, then? Is it very susceptible, Monsieur? Or is it really a matter for a physician?"

"Ah, Mademoiselle, can you ask? Can you doubt?"

My active toes were tickling gently all the time between his legs, where something very like a cucumber had gradually developed itself within the folds of his clothing.

"I am afraid your art is too much for you.

You are too much engrossed with fitting the ladies. Why not work for the men?"

"The men! Me! Dalmaine make boots for the beasts? I am not a merchant—*ferrant*—what you call him? *Farrier?* I do not make shoes for the horses! *Mon Dieu!* When I no longer make the *chaussures de dames,* I die! I go dead!"

In the agony of his disgust good Monsieur Dalmaine had seized my foot and ankle in his nervous grasp. He even emphasized his anguish by raising my leg until a portion of my calf was visible. I laughed so heartily that his confusion became even greater. Raising my other foot I almost pushed him backwards in my assumed merriment. Thus he had a chance of a private view, certainly not calculated to calm his excitement. His features proclaimed his delight. A sudden look of sensual pleasure spread over him as he saw my brown-stockinged legs. I let him enjoy the exhibition as long as he liked. My foot was all the time in contact with the cucumber. At last he could stand it no longer. He put down his hand. He himself pressed my little foot upon the most sensitive part.

"Ah, *Mon Dieu,* you are the most beautiful young lady I make for. You do not know what you make me suffer. When I see—when I feel these lovely little boots, I am made! When I make them I have pleasure. When I see them on your beautiful feet I go crack!"

I did not reply in words. I only raised my foot to his face as he knelt. He seized it again. He covered it with kisses. His white apron slipped to one side. The violent erection of his limb was plainly visible in his loose trousers. From the position he occupied I am sure he could see above my garters. I made no scruple in encouraging his passion.

"Poor Monsieur Dalmaine! Are you so very bad?"

"Oh, you most beautiful! I must fuck with you or burst! Oh dear! Oh dear!"

"I should be very sorry to make you suffer. Will it do you good, do you think?"

"I must fuck you! I must fuck! You are the angel of my dreams! I must feel—*il faut que je m'assoucisse avant de mourir!*"

His whole being quivered with excitement as he knelt, his hands convulsively clasping my ankles as I reclined in the easy chair.

"Are we quite sure not to be disturbed? Poor Monsieur Dalmaine, you shall not be disappointed. Only be prudent. Pray, do not hold my legs so high. How dreadfully indecent. Oh, really!"

"But first I must taste of your sweet *parfum*—of your essence divine. I must enjoy. Oh, yes! My beautiful young lady (clasping my foot in both hands) I have wanted you for a long time. Now!"

In another instant he had separated my legs. Plunging forward he had inserted his head between. He forcibly opened a passage. Before I could oppose any resistance to his attack, even had I been so inclined, his face was upon my naked thighs. He pressed forward. In pretending to protect myself, I assisted his design. With a stifled cry of delight he covered my parts with his lips. He drove in his long hot tongue. I felt him sucking my clitoris with all the fury of a satyr. The taste, the perfume appeared to drive him into a frenzy. Finding no further resistance, he clasped me around the loins. He continued his salacious gratification, steeping his mouth in the amorous secretion with which I liberally doused him. I was almost beside myself with the pleasure he was giving me. I spent continuously. Presently his right hand released me. I guessed his object. He raised himself from his recumbent position, but without quitting his vantage ground. His face was red and inflamed with lust. Raging desire had taken possession of the man. I had led him on. It was not in my power to stay him now, I had not long to wait. He tore open the front of his trousers. I saw his limb fiercely erect, red-capped and ready to do its work.

The lewd sight destroyed what little remained of prudence. I raised myself to favor his assault and he threw himself upon my willing body. Neither of us spoke but with a great gasp of acute delight I felt the stiff insertion of the Frenchman's long member into my parts.

Monsieur Dalmaine went to work at once. He was so fiercely charged with unappeased desire that he made all haste to quench his passion on me. In the midst of his desperate thrusts he took care to seize one of my feet in either hand. He thus had me at his mercy.

I felt his powerful movements within my belly where his limb was pushed as far as its great length could carry it. It was very strong and rigid. I enjoyed the act as much as he did. All too soon I knew he was about to discharge. He spent in a burst of semen which overflowed my parts. He sank groaning upon my bosom.

"Oh! Monsieur Dalmaine, is this what you call 'going crack'?"

CHAPTER 2

Our reduced establishment retired early. By 11 o'clock all the inmates had gone to their rooms for the night. Mrs. Lockett was heard to shut her door and turn the key. I thoroughly believe that John had purposely rusted that lock. Sometimes a drop of salt water is as useful as oil, in a different sense. At midnight the mansion was wrapped in slumber—all save John and I. At a quarter past 12 I admitted the footman. I lay with him that night. He entered noiselessly, as he had on felt slippers. I had thought of all. We were absolutely safe and alone. It was delicious to freely gratify one's voluptuous inclinations and indulge without restraint all one's libidinous ideas and conceptions. One great advantage was that under the circumstances John could mount me and moan to his heart's content without fear. My greedy nerves vibrated as I closed the door of

34

my chamber after the impatient good fellow. I motioned him to a seat. He submitted with the prompt obedience of a well-trained menial. Neither of us spoke. He watched me as I undressed.

I intentionally afforded him a delicious prospect. I saw his hands clench, his lips quiver, his nostrils dilate to his intoxications. I let fall my skirts. I stood in my chemise, my corset and my stockings. His greedy eyes followed every movement. I knew I was working the man into a state of almost unendurable longing. It was delightful to me. I grew excited beyond measure. I watched the keen, fierce, lecherous spirit overpowering all reserve—all prudence. I threw myself on the large couch.

"John, you may undress. I want to see you naked."

It had pleased me to act the schoolmistress in my intercourse with this man. It seemed to come natural to me. It served as a silly excuse for my precocious wantonness. It assuaged my amour proper. It gave me unbounded confidence in my character of an innocent led astray by the blandishment of a good-looking, full-grown man. John's natural vanity did the rest. To him I was the condescending young lady of the house seduced by his modest behavior, his rich livery. Above all, his manly proportions and his capacity for affording her sensuous delights.

I therefore looked on while John cast off his coat and divested himself of his striped garment underneath, depositing both within the adjoining room. Then came the turn of his scarlet breeches. I smiled at the semimodest, stupid air with which he let them fall. My mouth watered and my lips parted at the sight of his erect limb. His hairy belly and his shirt were raised.

"Come here, John, I want to feel your Robin."

In another minute my stallion was beside me. My eager hand closed around his huge member. I shook it and caressed it. I lowered my head and sucked it. It was delicious to my overwrought nerves. I took his big testicles in my grasp. I played with them.

"How shall we do it, John?"

"You'll let me do the job for you this time, won't you, Miss? Right into, I mean, Miss? I'll do it beautiful. You'll feel as if you were in heaven when Robin is pushing himself up and down your beautiful belly. It's all very well up against the door, standing up, but lying down with your sweet legs open he gets at it so free. He seems to get up almost to your waist."

As if to give point to his argument the rampant fellow opened my thighs. His face went between, his eager tongue inserted itself in my moist slit. I was in no humor to refuse him anything. I bore down on his thick, sensual lips. The scenes of the day came back to me. They passed as in a panorama before my closed eyes. John luxuriated in his prurient pleasure. I seemed to be exhaling for his delight the concentrated essence of previous luxury. The thought added poignancy to the sensations he caused me. I shivered with ecstasy.

"Oh, John, dear John . . . you are making me come!"

The delighted footman reveled in the solution of bygone pleasure with which I now liberally saturated him. I rose to my feet. Then I beheld his strong member, erect, redheaded, stiff as a bar of metal, threatening an onslaught upon my delicate person. I saw him gloating over my naked slit.

"Hush John. Whisper only. How shall we do it, dear John?"

He clasped me to him. He pressed his big, hairy chest to my tender form. He carried me towards the bed. He sat me upon it.

"Oh, Miss, let me do it so. Let me put it into you. See how stiff I am. It's bursting nearly. It's so full of the cream you are so fond of."

"So, John—on the side of the bed. Now push it into me. Oh! Oh, how big you are, John! Oh! Go slowly. It hurts."

Huge as it was, the big thing went in—up into me, till I felt the two big testicles pressing against my bottom. My stallion was at work upon me. The lewd fellow lolled back his head. He rolled his eyes in his luxury. His hands clutched nervously at my haunches as he pulled me towards him. Then he thrust slowly in and out—up and down in my little belly where he had said he longed to be.

I love to look on a man in this condition, filled with a fiery sense of unappeased desire, struggling in his libidinous embrace, his eyes turned up and burning with lust at the contemplation of the object of his passion extended at his mercy beneath him. The picture is a delicately fond one to my luxurious temperament—it enhances enormously my own enjoy-

37

ment. It is the sacrifice of modesty upon the altar of lust; it is the reversal of all that is reserved, becoming and dignified. It is this which is its charm. It is the utter abnegation of personal respect, the surrender of virtue to animal passion which is its fascination.

The enjoyment of my poor John came alas to its end as all things must. It grew too poignant to last and finally burst. I was the recipient of his exhausting efforts. He left me bathed in his essence to my intense enjoyment, and to his own loss.

* * *

"A telegram for you, Miss. I would not disturb you sooner. Fanny told me you had given orders not to be awakened."

"Oh, thank you, Mrs. Lockett; but I have been awake already a couple of hours. I have even had my tub, you see."

I tore open the telegram. It was from Eastbourne—from Percy.

"Mother has suffered a fresh attack, is extremely unwell. Lord L—— desires you to remain. Await further news."

The further news arrived an hour later. As I had anticipated, it was from the local medical practitioner.

"Lord L—— desires me to inform you that Lady L—— succumbed at three o'clock this morning. He begs you to be calm."

I pass over those particulars. They have no place here. Enough that Lady L—— had paid the inevitable price of her folly, and that poor

Papa was free. Sippett lost a profitable employment. I was told that her luggage was heavy and voluminous when she went away.

* * *

"A gentleman to see you, Miss. He says he has come on business. I told him you could see no one but he insisted. Here is his card."

"Mr. William Dragoon, Bow Street. Quite right, John. I will see this gentleman. Show him into Lord L——'s study. I will come up directly."

The blinds were drawn. The house gave the usual dolorous impression of Society grief. At such times one receives odd visitors, always in business, of course. It was not yet ten o'clock. The situation was already quite accustomed. Everyone went about his duties as usual, only speaking lower and looking solemn instead of simpering.

" I should not have called but that I thought I could do so without fear under the present circumstances. We had the news at six this morning direct from Bow Street."

"I am sure you are very good and you would not have come but for a useful object. I feel bewildered."

"I know—I know. Do not trouble to explain. I only want to caution you. Of course I know your position is a little difficult. Take my advice, will you? That's right. I knew you would —for it is honest. Do not delay your marriage. Listen to me: I told you, little beauty, once, not so long ago, your fortune lies at your feet.

39

You have only to stoop to win it. It lies so still. But you must act."

"How do you mean? What must I do?"

Dragoon looked cautiously around. He even closed the slide over the keyhole. He waited a moment and listened acutely.

"I know much more than you think. Your groom is not to be trusted. Young men are vain and they boast. He is steady but he is no better than his fellows. You have elected to pick up what lay at your feet. Another trouble arises. Women are plotting. They are devils when they are jealous. Do not delay on account of what has happened. Try to shorten time. Lord Endover is surrounded by interesting women. Women are in his councils also. You are quite safe yet. Strike while the iron is hot; you know what I mean. Do not give him time to let them get at him. They will ruin you if they can."

He looked at me appealingly. His manner was most respectful.

"I really hardly see and yet—I know you are good and honest in what you say. Frankly, I will take your advice. You frighten me. I thought I was so safe—so guarded."

"So you are *as yet*. That is why I have come to reassure you and to caution you. I know all that passes at Endover. Take my advice. And now, good-bye. Look all the facts in the face—*and marry him quick*."

Dragoon rose. He bowed with an almost mock solemnity which had its significance. In another moment he was gone.

The day passed wearily enough. In the afternoon Lord Endover called. He was all sympathy for me and condolence. His passion was evidently at its zenith. He regarded me as the object of his most cherished desires. The position was difficult. I told him I had not yet seen my Papa. I would consult him. My fiancé was evidently alarmed lest a long delay should be added to his probation. He had my permission to return the day following. I told him he was welcome. I said I desired his companionship and his advice. He left me much pleased and flattered.

I passed the evening with Mrs. Lockett. She brought her needlework to my sitting room. At an early hour I retired to rest. She supplied the place of my maid. I had never known the tender offices of a mother. I was grateful for her sympathy. I cried myself to sleep.

When I rose the next morning I had resolved all my difficulties. I had also carefully laid my plans. I prepared to put them into execution.

For malignity there is no expression to equal the intensity of the simply pronoun, "she," when hissed through the lips in an undertone as another woman speaks of a member of her sex behind her back. It conveys not only the absence of all respect, but the full measure of contempt which can be brought to bear on the absent one.

I felt I was being discussed and probably in quarters where I desired to be at my best. I felt quite equal to the occasion, but there was no time to be lost. I resolved to act at once. Thanks to Dragoon, I was warned and therefore armed.

41

* * *

"Ah, what a pleasure! I never expected to see you, my lovely one, this morning—and so early too. Why, business has been so dull lately that I have closed quite early. The season is a lot too good for us doctors; no colds, no bronchitis. What is London coming to! But you look anxious and not quite so well as usual."

"Well, I am glad to see you, all the same. I am not quite so well, perhaps, as usual. I have had bad news. No, do not ask me about it. You remember our compact; it is because I rely on your word of honor that I am here. I want your advice. I have lost a relative. But that is not the immediate cause of my visit. It has raised complications. I am uncertain what to do for the best."

My tall, fair young disciple of Esculapius consigned the care of his establishment to his lad. He ushered me into his back parlor with a look of radiant delight on his handsome face.

"Now, my beautiful. Tell me how I can be of use. I am entirely at your service. I hope the matter is not very grave. You look weary."

"You remember the conclusions you arrived at regarding the difficulty in the way of . . . of . . . well, I need not be reserved with you, my friend: I mean in the way of conception?"

"Certainly I do and I am still of that opinion. I am absolutely certain that every physician who took the same pains in the examination and who was proficient in his practice would confirm them."

"Then you are still sure I could not bear a child to my husband if I married?"

"Quite sure—and for the matter of that—to no one else."

"But that if I submitted myself to an operation—a slight operation—in that case, I should have the same chance as other healthy young women?"

"Exactly so. I believe more than an even chance, because you are so beautifully, so perfectly formed. Without going into professional particulars, let me tell you: you should sit to a friend of mine who is an artist—as our Mother Eve—for your figure is the perfection of all that is desirable for the procreation of the race."

"Oh, you wicked serpent! But seriously, is that your solemn declaration? Much may depend on your reply."

"It is, my Eve, my most serious opinion. Which you may have confirmed any day you please."

He had placed me in his easy chair. He now came and sat beside me. His face wore an anxious and dejected look.

"So you are going to be married. I might have guessed that so beautiful a girl with so much self-possession, forgive me for saying so, with so much force of character, would not be long without the choice of husbands."

"You may be right, but what then? We are already good friends."

"There, my darling, we are already good friends and if I could think—well, let me explain—if you would not give me up altogether, but if you would come to me sometimes, I, well . . . I should not be jealous."

I felt piqued. I hardly know why. He seemed

43

almost to catch at the idea of my marrying as something to be desired, and yet he was not at his ease. He waited a moment. He evidently saw my perplexity. Then he continued.

"To be plain with you, my sweet little girl, you are the most delicious treat I ever had in all my life. I have always fancied married women. If only you were really married you would drive me mad with lust to enjoy you. Your enchantment would simply be doubled."

"Is that so? If that is your whim, I will not fail to gratify it. You shall have me all to yourself as soon after I am married as I can contrive it. Are you satisfied?"

He took me in his arms. He became furiously indecent. His face, his voice, his movements, all united to betray the desire which raged within him.

"Oh, my darling! My love! You have given me such pleasure. You promise me? You will let me have you after your marriage?"

"I promise."

We were standing face to face. He pushed me towards the wall. He pressed himself lewdly upon me. He covered my face with hot kisses and took me in his arms. In a second his trousers were open and my hand closed on his limb.

"Oh, how stiff you are! What a size! Do you really like married women? Are they so nice? Is it part of your enjoyment to know that you are committing a real adultery?"

"It is awfully delicious to enjoy a married woman. Your promise maddens me. I consider you are one already. Come, let me have you. I must! I want you so badly. What lovely legs! Don't try to stop my hand. Oh, yes, skin back my thing. It is so nice. Your fingers are so warm and soft. Kiss me! Give me your tongue. You would like to suck it? So then, take it between your pretty lips. What a stupid fool your husband must be! I am going to spend into his wife's belly."

He seized me in his arms. He lifted me panting with my lips exhaling the ambrosia of his large tool. He laid me on the sofa. He was evidently madly excited by his strangely lecherous idea. I determined to encourage it.

"But what would he say? I am his property now; I really cannot let you abuse me. Oh, stop! Fie, take your hands away! Oh . . . you are strong, so cruel to me."

He forced me down. He pressed his long and powerful form upon me. My thighs were easily parted. His stiff limb wagged between them. I felt him divide the moist lips. The next moment he was into me.

"Oh, Christ, what a lovely girl you are! How tight it is! There! There! Now take it quite in. Does that please you? Is that better than your husband's? What a fool! I am going to spend into his wife."

"Oh, shameful! Let me go . . . you must take it out. You must not finish. What would he say? Don't you know you are committing adultery?"

"Yes, that's it. Adultery! Ah, how tight you are! My little married friend. No! No! I shall not take it out. I shall spend into you. Do you hear? Right into your delicious little womb."

"Oh, my poor husband. You are killing me with your great thing. What will he say. Oh!

Oh! You are going to spend. You are coming. Oh, so am I."

* * *

A few hours later my wedding was fixed to take place in a few months. Lord Endover left me in a transport of pleasure. He declared his intention to come very frequently if I would allow him to do so. I was most amiable. He received every assurance of my affectionate consideration.

I think I have already demonstrated that I am a hypocrite. The difference is only in degree; the necessity is universal. I never care to do things by halves. I am therefore a very great hypocrite. The higher your position in Society, the more consummate must be your hypocrisy. The attribute begins with the highest. Is not every evasion of the truth a smooth, a plausable hypocrisy? Nobody believes it all the same; that is the strangest part of it. It is offered and accepted. Everybody excuses it, weighs it at its own fictitious value and passes it on. "Tell the truth and shame the devil," that somewhat shabby proverb goes. I think, after a careful study of the subject, that Society would be much more ashamed, in spite of its usual regard, or rather lack of regard of that sentiment, if it had to tell the truth. Weighing one opinion with another, I fancy His Satanic Majesty is decidedly in the background. He could set to work to render his own Society so much more select if he only would— there being so much material to choose from.

A just sense of the value of hypocrisy, of

its judicious use, is absolutely necessary if you would shine in the flickering light of Society. Yet I am not afraid of criticism. I defy criticism to do me any harm. It would certainly not do me any good. No more than Marie Corelli herself. But I have no necessity to rack my brains to produce Demons and Divinities. I find in my exalted position enough of both in Society itself. I meet in every salon, in every boudoir, the saintly who cannot keep his fingers off his choristers; the elderly lordling who apes the vices of a Domitian or a Nero; the minister of religion who ministers to the lambs of his flock in more senses than one; and the blatant, pretentious man-about-town who divides his time and attention between his exaggerated shirt collar and his simpering partner. He would delight to be the very devil himself, if he only knew how. There are, too, the lonely, loving hearts, who, in the never resting vortex, watch long and sadly for the coming of the one they dreamed of the sad long days ago, or who mourn unceasingly the one who will never return, whose hopes never flag, whose faith is intact beneath the false mask they must wear and who will be as constant as I shall be to give up all, to submit to the inevitable when it comes.

CHAPTER 3

"At last I have my darling girl with me again. It has been quite a terrible time, my dear Eveline. You are quite right to remain in town as I directed."

"My dear Papa had only to express his wishes. Eveline is always ready to gratify them."

"I hope you got on well in this lonely house, my dear child."

"Yes, Papa, Mrs. Lockett was very sympathetic. John got on too very nicely. I managed to keep things together. He felt acutely."

Over a week passed since the news had reached me. All was quite over now. The house resumed its wonted appearance. Lord L—— had returned. Percy was at the depot. Only our somber costumes which conventional habit enjoins betrayed to outsiders the change which had taken place so recently.

"You have brought Johnson back with you, of course, my dear Papa? How is Gurkha? Does he look after him? Do you know, Papa, I am not over pleased with Jim, as you call him."

"Why so, Eveline? I thought he was rather a favorite of yours."

"Yes, well . . . he was . . . but to tell the truth, I mistrust that young man Johnson. I believe he is inquisitive. I had occasion more than once to be careful when you and I were riding together, dear Papa. He tries to overhear our conversation. I am sure of that."

"Is that so? Then Jim must go."

"Didn't I see your old friend Sir Currie Fowles who was going out to take up his new appointment in Madras?"

"By Jove, yes. And he asked me to look him out a groom. He wants one to take out with him. He knows I am like him, averse to native syces and prefer an Englishman in charge of my stables in India, so he came to me. Johnson would suit him exactly. I will see to this at once."

Ten days later Jim was tending horses on board a P & O mail steamer in the Red Sea, as head groom to the new Vice Consul in Madras. He received a considerable advance in wages and I was well rid of him.

We sat close together. We spoke of the future. I explained the arrangement for the wedding and told Lord L—— that I had fixed the date. He willingly assented to all. He said it had his entire approval, and that Lord Endover had already written to him on the subject. We could not help feeling that we were

49

now thrown together more than ever. The sentiment of mutual confidence had become stronger as he spoke of my forthcoming marriage. I thought I detected a certain feeling of jealousy in it which pained me.

"We shall always be the same to each other as we are, dear Papa. Shall we not? Nothing shall ever change your little girl as regards her love for you, dear."

"My only anxiety is that no harm shall befall you, my dearest child; no awkward contretemps should take place before your future is assured."

"Have no fear on that account, darling Papa. All is quite safe and will continue so."

"Where are you going, Eveline? That black silk bodice becomes you charmingly."

"I was going to my bootmaker, dear Papa. I want some more black kid boots."

"Extravagant little puss! Why those you are wearing are lovely."

"Do you like them? See, they do not fit badly. What do you think?"

I turned my foot about to show him. I raised my skirt sufficiently to show off my dainty calf in its glistening silk stocking as well.

"By heaven, my dear child, you tempt me dreadfully."

He caught me in his arms. He set me on his knee. With a trembling hand he fondled both boot and leg. Our lips met in a long hot embrace.

"What is to stop you, dear Papa? Certainly not your Eveline."

His excitement increased. We were safe in his room. I was sure of him now. I wanted it badly. He could see the flames of lust in my eyes. He drew me still closer. I put my hand on his trousers. His limb was quite stiff. It was so long since I had felt it; so long since it had been my enjoyment. His pent up passion betrayed itself in every muscle of his face, in every movement of his nervous frame. He put me off his knee and stood before me.

"Oh, Eveline child, I must have you at once. We have a good chance. Oh, my God! How long I have waited for your enjoyment. How I pant for the pleasure we shall give each other."

His passion rose as he spoke. He threw his arms about me. I unbuttoned his trousers. I caressed his handsome limb in my new black kid glove. Papa glared at the lewd spectacle as my little hand moved up and down the standing object in my grasp.

"Is this dear thing so bad, dear Papa? Eveline will take it and comfort it. It shall have all the delightful things it wants. We are alone. Let us do all that will give us the most pleasure."

I put my lips to his ear. I whispered so indecent an invitation that with a low exclamation of lascivious frenzy he bore me towards the sofa and raised my clothes. I fell backwards. He fell upon me. I was all aswim with longing for the incestuous encounter. I guided the skinny knob of his thing to my eager parts. The strong and erect instrument slipped voluptuously into me. He positively foamed at the mouth in his agony of enjoyment. For a few seconds no sound was heard but his stentorian breathing and the rustle of my black

51

silk dress. My spasms became delicious. My womb seemed to open to him invitingly. His limb hardened throughout its length. He discharged with a low groan of rapture. I received every drop of his thick seed—the seed from which I was made. When he retired I kissed off the slippery exuberance of his spendings from the end of his drooping limb. I rearranged the disorder of my condition, baptized as I was with his rich sperm.

I made my preparations to go out. I went alone. The cab set me down at the corner of Great Castle Street. I entered the shop of Monsieur Dalmaine. I had made an appointment with the artist bootmaker.

"Good morning, Monsieur Dalmaine. Are my new boots ready?"

"But certainly, Mademoiselle. Am I not always of the most exact? Besides, how can I keep waiting my most beautiful client?"

"Let us try them on."

He led me into the back room beyond which was his atelier. I seated myself in the large chair. Dalmaine produced the boots from a glass case. He held up these for my inspection. His little eyes danced with pleasure as he scrutinized the glossy black *peau de cheveiul* and the exquisite work of his skilled assistants.

"They appear perfect. I trust they are not too tight. Not like *souliers de vingt-cinq*—you know."

"They are the correct fit for your lovely foot, Mademoiselle. I know not what *souliers de vingt-cinq* are. What are they?"

52

"They are *neuf et trois*, Monsieur Dalmaine: consequently they are *vingt-cinq*."

"Ah, *Mon Dieu!* Now only do I discover you! It is too good—*neuf et tres et trois! Mais c'est splendide!*"

He sank at my feet. He removed my boot. He inserted my toe into the new one. I pushed my other foot against his apron. The cucumber was already in evidence. I could feel its magnificent proportions. Meanwhile, without noticing my proceedings, the artist in ladies' boots became wholly absorbed in the elegance and delicate fit of his darling study. He no sooner had my foot in than he began lacing in the most exact manner, his face beaming with smiles as he drew the laces together. Not a sign escaped him to show that I had ever permitted any undue familiarity. Nothing marked his conduct beyond the most respectful attention to do credit to his employment.

"I think you had better put on the other boot also, please, so as to make sure there is nothing amiss."

He trembled with delight as he held the pair on my feet. He molded them, he fondled them alternately. I pushed my right foot towards the cucumber, now evidently getting beyond control.

"Ah, Mademoiselle. It is too much! You make me so bad. It is not possible to resist. You are so beautiful."

He pushed his hand away up on my leg. He lost suddenly all his reserve. His other hand was engaged in releasing his member. He turned up my dress as carefully as if he were my own maid. I saw him fix his gaze on my

53

thighs. His fingers pressed on higher yet. He met with no restraint. Suddenly he pushed forward and his face was pressed upon my naked legs. He continued until his head was quite buried beneath my clothes. He gained ground and found his way to the central spot of his desire. I felt him seize the coveted spot with an exclamation of rapture. I pressed his naked limb between my feet. I parted my legs to give him room. His large tongue was now rolling on and around my clitoris, already excited and swollen with the previous exercise Papa had given it. He gave me delicious pleasure. I pressed down upon him, continually responding to his amorous caress with renewed effusions. At length I drew back. He raised his streaming lips. He pulled aside his white apron. I saw his huge member, red-capped and shining stiff as a bar of ivory, distended in front of me.

I gloated on the luscious morsel before me. It resembled John's. It was just as handsome. I seized it. I fingered it all about.

"Stand up. It is my turn now."

The excited man obeyed only too willingly. The stiff limb was within a few inches of my face. I examined it thoroughly. I pressed back the thick white covering skin which lay around the glistening head.

"So this is what you go 'crack' with, Monsieur Dalmaine!"

He was apparently too engrossed to reply. He glanced towards the shop door. He saw that the bolt was shot. All was quiet. He smiled. I imprinted a moist kiss on the little opening in the head.

54

"Oh, *Mon Dieu!* Mademoiselle! You will drive me to the mad!"

I repeated those moist kisses; my pointed tongue took part in the salacious game. The cucumber acknowledged my condescension by stretching its warm length eagerly to my caress.

I delighted to watch the voluptuous effects on my companion. I continued my kisses; my tickling touches; I worked my little hands in unison.

With the instinct of his countrymen he divined my intention. He still further loosened his clothing and drew back his shirt and trousers. He exposed his belly, his thick bush of sandy hair, his large testicles, closely drawn up between his standing member. I noted all. I determined to gratify him to the utmost. My whole being vibrated with prurient exultation at the delicious prosepct. He pushed his loins forward. My lips opened until they engulfed the head of his limb.

"Ah, *quel plaisir!* You are giving me the pleasure celestial!"

The contact, pressure and suction of my lips seemed to madden, to frenzy. To say he enjoyed conveys but a faint notion of his condition. His eyes were half-closed or fixed alternately on my face. His breath came in gasping sobs. He was acutely sensible of the delicious friction I was providing for him. I continued my voluptuous task. He replied with gentle pushes which served to thrust his stiff limb backwards and forwards upon my tongue. My fingers worked steadily along the white shaft. I stopped suddenly. I drew back. It was the pleasure of anticipation. I looked on the throbbing member close to my lips.

"Do you like that? Is it nice? Say if I shall recommence."

"Ah, Mademoiselle, you are so kind! You give me such pleasure!"

"Would you like me to finish like that?"

"Ah, but yes, sweet Mademoiselle! Make me to finish in your pretty mouth."

"Oh, you shocking, naughty man! What! You want to make that thing finish in a lady's mouth?"

"Yes, yes! I will give you pleasure also."

"You have already afforded me pleasure. I shall, if this pleases you, recommence. I am ready to gratify you."

"Ah, *Mon Dieu!* I shall be quick! I shall have the pleasure of the immortal gods!"

Even as he spoke he pushed the broad head of his thing between my lips. I sucked it voraciously while my gloved hand caressed and stroked the shaft. Dalmaine bent forward. He placed his hands on the back of an easy chair. I took all I could manage of his big member. The game was too good to last long. He gave a little cry. He pushed forward. The next instant my throat and mouth were filled with a flood of sperm. I was greedy. The hot spurts followed each other in quick succession until all was over. I rejected nothing. We had mutually gratified each other's perverse desires.

*   *   *

It rained for the best part of two days. London was out of season. Only the necessity of

56

making preparations for my approaching nuptials kept Lord L—— and myself in town. I began to feel the insupportable ennui and lassitude which causes one only to fly to almost any distraction to escape from it. Papa remarked on my dejection. He attributed it to the right cause. He was always shrewd in care of me. Divining a means of relief, he hastened to make his proposition.

"You remember, my darling Eveline, our conversation at Eastbourne, when I proposed that a pleasure of unusual delight awaited you?"

"Oh, yes, dear Papa, certainly I do. Only our preoccupation has prevented my curiosity from becoming importunate. What is it to be? When am I to make this new experience?"

"We have nothing in particular to do this evening, dear child. I propose we spend it in the indulgence of this pleasure."

"Oh, Papa, that would be lovely. To tell the truth I am dreadfully dull and ready for anything. Besides, you told me it was medicine for me."

"So be it then! We will dine half an hour earlier than usual and sally forth together. All can be in readiness. I will complete the necessary arrangements at once."

"Dear, kind, Papa! You are always thinking of your little loving Eveline. You are feeling dull, too, and not looking so well as usual."

"We will have a dose of sensuality that will rouse us both."

"Indeed we will! I already feel better. I will go and put on my most enticing things to please my dear Papa."

57

I had time to make my toilet before the afternoon tea was served. John brought it in. Lord L—— had gone out. I well knew his errand. The footman shut the door, drew down the blinds and placed a chair at the table for my convenience. We were all alone.

"It is three whole days since you noticed poor Robin, Miss Eveline."

"So it is, John. Bring him here—pull him out."

In another second John had his limb out. It showed quite red and white against the black hair on his belly. It was half erect already. The perfume of the male organ began to excite my senses. I laid hold of it. I kissed it— I sucked it for a moment. It rose, superb and rampant at the contact of my warm lips. Then I stopped.

"Not now, dear John, perhaps tonight or tomorrow night, upstairs, I will give you a chance. I am not in the humor now."

The man looked disappointed. I thought him even surly. It occurred to me that I might not be wise to continue this liaison. Was it not time to break it off? Mischief might come of it.

John put away his unhappy member. He buttoned his plush breeches. I thought I caught the muttered words: "A reason for that, perhaps?" as he left the room.

Lord L—— had returned in excellent time for dinner. I could see by his cheerful manner that he had reasons to be content with himself and his mission.

"All is arranged and will be ready. We will

be as secret as the stones of Troy. You will see all in good time. How ravishing you look!"

I wore a black satin bodice and skirt trimmed with black lace, somewhat open in the front and exposing the upper roundness of my bosom. My hair was simply caught up with pins and twisted behind. It was well secured. Black silk openwork stockings of a very fine material, black glossy kid gloves, very thin and with very soft and high French heels, set off my little feet and ankles. The rest was duly arranged as I knew he loved to have it.

We drove to a second-rate theater. Lord L—— sent the brougham home. We slipped out again. Papa took me in his arms, then we threaded more than one small street. We made sure we were not observed. Then suddenly we started again. A door opened—we entered a house. I thought I knew the place. I had been there with Dragoon.

We went upstairs. A little woman in black pushed open a door. I found myself in a narrow corridor. About six feet in front was another door. A third door was on the left. The right hand side was apparently a blank wall. Lord L—— himself pushed open the door immediately in front. It gave access to an elegantly furnished chamber. A soft light came from the screened yellow light which hung suspended from the center. There were pictures on the walls. Two rather handsomely carved wood brackets occupied places on the side of the doorway. On them were two heavy vases.

"Here is a delightful little temple of pleasure, Eveline. The place is so secret and re-

59

tired that it has never yet been disturbed by vestries or police."

I kept my ideas to myself. I waited for more.

"It is here that I have arranged for your medicine. The substantial medicine that you require dear girl, I have ordered. To drop all metaphor, you will meet here a fine young fellow whose very conditions preclude all risk. His actions are circumscribed. He is, as I told you, both deaf and dumb. He was so born."

"Poor fellow. I do not think I shall be afraid of him. Is he—is he very nice, dear Papa? So very strong—you know what I mean."

"My informant is a medical man—a member of my club. In the course of a conversation he related the case to me. He tells me he is possessed with a surprising degree of copulative power. I was told how I might see him nude and I went to a public bath. I soon picked him out. He was a study for a sculpture. And, oh, my darling girl . . . what a lovestick!"

I have the habit of blushing when I like. I did it then. It is not difficult when you know how.

"Here is a luxurious bed, Eveline. I wish you all the pleasure you are capable of in this retreat of sensuality. I shall come and fetch you when all is over. Meanwhile I will not be far off. You are quite safe here. You can make yourself quite at your ease. You have nothing to fear and all to enjoy, my darling. I will send him up. His name is Theodore."

He left the room. I heard him close both doors. Almost immediately Theodore made his appearance. I was at once struck by this young fellow's really and truly distinguished appearance. His seeming awkwardness of manner was evidently due to so unusual an introduction, but his bearing, his personality, were conspicuous. They were more. They were most uncommon.

He was rather more than fair. His height could not have been less than six feet two inches. His hair of rich auburn was naturally curly and glossy. His complexion was clear and bright. His eyes remarkably fine and expressive. Poor fellow! It was sad to think he neither heard a human voice nor expressed his ideas in speech. His individuality, however, compensated in some measure for these defects.

He came straight up to me with a rather weak smile on his face, as if he were shy. So, in truth, I found him. I motioned him to sit down by me. I made room for him on the sofa. I noticed how he watched furtively all my movements and seemed to be impressed by my personal appearance.

"You are a very handsome young man."

There was no answer. He produced an elaborately mounted slate on which was attached a crayon and a sponge.

I remembered my mistake. I wrote my remark on the slate. He broke into an intelligent smile at once. His whole being seemed to awake in response to my sentence. He was evidently vain. Poor fellow! He commenced writing rapidly. I followed his pencil with my eyes.

"Nature has not been wholly unkind to me.

I am strong. I am young. I rejoice in life. I have the means to enjoy it."

I smiled and put my left hand on his shoulder. I wrote:

"Can you make love?"

"It would not be difficult for anyone to love you. I could die for a girl like you. I have never seen a more beautiful woman."

"Are you in earnest? Would you really like to make love to me?"

In an instant his arms were around me. His lips pressed to mine. His breath was sweet as an angel's. His eyes shone into mine with the awakening of uncontrollable desire. He wrote rapidly:

"I love you already, you are so sweet. I want you. Will you let me?"

I took up the crayon.

"We are here to make love together."

Again there was no use for the slate. He pressed my form to his. He thrust his trembling hands toward my bosom. I denied him nothing. He panted. It was plain he was becoming more and more excited. He covered my face, my neck, my hands with burning kisses. Love and desire have no need for words. It is a language quite understood without sound, communicated without speech. He felt its intensity. Its influence brought with it an unsupportable necessity for relief. He wrote quickly on the slate:

"Do I make myself clear? I possess unusual advantages with which to please a beautiful and voluptuous girl like you."

I read. I believed and blushed. I playfully pulled his ear. He kissed me on the mouth in

62

mock revenge. He became enterprising. He essayed familiarities which were hardly decent. I feigned sufficient resistance to flame his rising fancy. Suddenly he released me again to write:

"I conclude there is no need for too much modesty between us to interfere with our mutual pleasures?"

"No. I am here for your pleasure. You are here for mine. We should enjoy each other. Let us make love in earnest."

His eyes shot flames of lust. He took the slate.

"You are no less sensual than beautiful. We will drown ourselves in pleasure. I love pleasure. With you it will be divine."

He threw off his coat. He assisted me to remove my bodice. Soon I stood in my corset of pale blue satin and a short skirt of the same color and material. He rapidly divested himself of his outer things. He caught my hand. He carried it under his shirt.

"Oh, good heavens! What a monster!"

His instrument was as long as John's and it was even thicker. It was stiff as a ramrod and it throbbed under my touches. He pressed my hand upon it and laughed a strange silent laugh. Then he wrote on the slate.

"What do you call that?"

This was evidently a challenge. Nothing bashful, I took it up at once.

"I call it an instrument—a weapon of offense, a limb."

He put his left hand between my thighs as he wrote:

"I call it a cock."

63

"Well, he certainly has a very fine crest. He carries himself very proudly. His head is as red as a turkey-cock's. He is a real beauty."

The slate was thrown on one side. Theodore drew me on his knees. He tucked up my short, lace trimmed chemise. I made only just enough resistance to whet his appetite. He lifted me in his strong arms like a child. He bore me to the bed. He deposited me gently upon it. He was by my side in a moment, minus everything but his shirt, which stuck up in front of him as if it were suspended on a peg—as indeed it was. Theodore laid his handsome head on my breast. He toyed with my most secret charms. My round and plump posteriors seemed especially to delight him. I grasped his enormous member in my hand. I ventured also to examine the heavy purse which hung below. His testicles were in proportion to his splendid limb. I separated them from each other. There seemed to be something I did not understand. I felt them over again. Surely . . . yes . . . I was correct. He had three! He led me eagerly to the soft couch.

Once there he recommenced his amorous caresses. I seized him once more by his truncheon. It was so nice to feel the warm length of flesh—the broad red nut, the long white shaft and the triangle of testicles which were drawn up so tight below it. It was so strange, too, that this young man could neither hear nor speak. The spirit of mischief took possession of me. The demon of lust vied with him in stimulating my passion.

I slipped off the bed. Theodore followed me. I raised my chemise up to my middle and laughingly challenged him to follow. The view of my naked charms was evidently appetizing. He tried to seize me again. I avoided his grasp. He ran after me around the table which stood at one end of the room. His expression was all frolic and fun, but with a strong tinge of sensuous desire in his humid eyes and moist lips. I let him catch me. He held me tight this time. I turned my back to him. I felt him pressing his brown curls on the hairy parts of my plump buttocks. He pushed me before him towards the bed. His huge member inserted itself between my thighs. I put my hand down to it. To my surprise he had placed an ivory napkin ring over it. It reduced the available length. It certainly left me less to fear from its unusually large proportions. I had already taken the precaution to anoint my parts with cold cream. I adjusted the head as I leaned forward, belly down on the bed. The young fellow pushed. He entered. I thought he would split me up. He held me by the hips and thrust it into me. It passed up. I groaned with a mingled feeling of pain and pleasure.

He was too excited to pause now. He bore forward, setting himself solidly to work to do the job. I passed my hand down to feel his cock, as he called it, as it emerged from time to time from the pliable sheath. Although I knew he could not hear, yet it delighted me to utter my sensation. Women must talk; they can't help it. I was every bit a woman at that moment. Besides, I could express my ideas in any language I liked, as crudely as I chose;

65

there was no one to hear me, no one to offend, no one to chide. I jerked forward.

"Oh, take it out. Don't spend yet. I want to change. It's so delicious. How sweetly you poke me, my dear fellow!"

The huge instrument extricated itself with a plop. Theodore divined my intention. He aided me to place myself upon the side of the bed. I took his cock in my hand. I examined it avidly. It was lovely now—all shining and glistening, distended and rigid.

"I want it all . . . all . . . all!"

He understood. He slipped off the napkin ring. He presented it again to my eager slit. It went up slowly.

"Oh, my God! It is too long now! Oh! Oh! Never mind . . . give me it all! Ah, go slowly . . . you brute . . . you are splitting me! Do you hear! Oh! Push now . . . I'm coming!"

He perceived my condition. He bore up close to me as long as my emitting spasms lasted. My swollen clitoris was in closest contact with the back of his staff, which tickled deliciously.

I clung to him with both thighs. I raised my belly to meet his stabbing thrusts. I seized the pillow and covered my face. I bit the pillowcase in my frenzy. When I had finished he stopped a little to let me breathe.

"You have not come, but you will soon. I know it. I can feel it by the strong throbbing of your cock. I want it . . . oh, I want it! I must hold your balls while you spend. I want your sperm."

He became more and more urgent. He was having me with all his tremendous vigor. His strokes were shorter, quicker. My thighs worked in unison. His features writhed in his ecstasy of enjoyment. He was nearing the end. I felt every throb of his huge instrument.

I draw the veil over the termination of the scene. I cannot even use ordinary terms to describe it. My whole nervous system vibrated with voluptuous excitement. My senses deserted me.

When I recovered consciousness, to my astonishment, my companion had disappeared. Papa was standing over my prostrate form. How he had been occupied I shall never know. His face was turgid with satisfied lust. His hands trembled. His dress was disordered. He held in his hands a towel with which he was bathing my aching parts.

He assisted me at my toilet. As I passed out with Lord L—— I noticed that the door on the left of the little corridor was ajar. I peeped through. It gave me access to a little cabinet, not larger than the inside of a double brougham. In the partition which separated it from the chamber where my adventure had taken place, there was one bright point of light which shone from a round hole the size of a wine cork. A hasty glance explained all. The carved fretwork of the bracket on which stood all vases was perforated just under the shelf and quite invisible from that side. I understood all.

Lord L—— had witnessed the activities that had taken place. I hastily followed Papa, who had already descended the stairs. He waited for me. I am not a fool. I kept my discovery to myself.

CHAPTER 4

Wedding bells! The usual bustle and fuss. The usual ceremony. The usual lies on both sides. The usual hypocritical admiration of everybody for everybody, and behold, the day had come! In fact, was half gone when I was made the Countess of Endover.

The marriage ceremony was necessarily a quiet one. It was made as short as possible. A few intimate friends appeared at the church. The dear old Duchess of M—— insisted on being there. She was one of the few whose compliments were not all flattery.

Lord Endover really looked almost handsome in his uniform as Lord Lieutenant of the County. Papa and Percy paid him the honor of acknowledging his military standing as Lieutenant Colonel of Militia by also arraying themselves in their state panoply of war.

The three sisters of the husband were present, of course. The honorable Maud, a confirmed old maid; the next a widow, Lady Tintackle; the youngest, plain, spiteful and nine and twenty, yet a spinster, with every chance of remaining so—Margaret by name. She had begun life with one or two notorious escapades, from the results of which nothing but her brother's influence and position had saved her. The wave of disdain with which Society overwhelms offenders flagrantly transgressing its unwritten laws, and been detected, never seemed to quite unruffle her future. The men were all shy. All three sisters regarded me with little favor, jealous already of a new influence asserting itself between their brother and themselves. I foresaw great need of caution in my intercourse with my noble connections.

We were all relieved to get home. Lord Endover and Papa were closeted in the latter's study with the family solicitors. The ladies were whiling away the half hour before breakfast in the big drawing room. I had found an excuse to escape to my room. I bolted the door and sat down in my favorite chair before the looking glass. I was engaged in admiring myself in my beautiful wedding gown. I was glad to be alone. I wanted to think. I had many ideas to arrange.

We were to spend our honeymoon—how I hated the word!—at Endover Towers. The state rooms had been specially prepared. The place was said to be arranging a festive reception for the Earl and his young bride. The village was *enfete*. It was all to be very gorgeous and gay.

I was still before the mirror. Five minutes had not gone since my entry. Already there was a tap at the door. I rose and opened it. My brother Percy pushed his way in. He immediately locked the door again.

"Now I shall at least have a private view."

"What do you mean, you naughty boy?"

"Oh, it's no use riding the high horse with me, little Countess. Your Ladyship will please descend to the level of ordinary life."

He had seized me by the wrist. His other arm was around my waist in an instant.

"Oh, Percy, please, please, leave me alone! Someone may come!"

"I'm going to give the new Countess of Endover her first lesson in—why, you have no drawers on!"

"You really must not tumble my dress, Percy! For shame!"

He had put me before the large armchair. Before I could prevent him I was made to kneel in it. He had begun raising my skirts from behind. All protestations were in vain. I was horribly in fear someone would want to come in. Still, nothing was more natural than that my brother should come to offer me his private congratulations. He had only seen me once before that day in the church. We had scarcely exchanged a word.

"Oh Eve! Eve, dear! I've sworn to have you first after your marriage. I will not be denied. You looked divine at the altar. Like an innocent angel of light. I declare I could hardly keep my buttons on my trousers. Turn your head, dear Eve, and look."

I did as I was bidden; all power of resis-

70

tance seemed to pass away. What I saw fired my hot blood.

"Oh, Percy, you wicked boy! It is bigger and bigger. Make haste then. I shall have to go downstairs in a minute."

He pressed his belly to my bottom. My wedding dress and underskirts were thrown over my head. In another instant he was in me up to the balls. There was no time to lose. He knew it. He worked fast to arrive at his climax. My own arrived quickly. With a low groan I sank my head on the cushioned back. His weapon straightened, hardened, and with a sigh he discharged.

Ten minutes later I entered the drawing room. Breakfast was announced. Lord Endover was complimented on all sides. He disposed of my beautiful bouquet on a side table. There was no fuss. There were no speeches—only our healths and champagne.

That evening at 5:30 we entered the village and drove to the towers. The local volunteers with their band bade us welcome at the station. All was in readiness for our reception at Lord Endover's noble country seat. It was a grand old pile. The family had bought it some two hundred years before from the original noble family that had held it since the time of William.

I pass over that portion of my history which relates to my early married life. I am not a hypocrite from choice but from the necessities of my position. Lord Endover never relaxed his fondness for me. I became disgusted with myself. Incapable of reciprocating his passion, I sought a retreat in our beautiful country seat in Cumberland. The Autumn season of Parliament had been started. There were weighty political issues in the balance; my husband had to be present.

It was then that I heard sad tidings from my old home in —— Street, Mayfair. Lord L—— wrote often. In one of his letters he told me that John, the footman, having been sent to St. John's Wood on an important message had met with an accident. He had been run over by a cab and was badly hurt. Conveyed to a hospital, he never quite recovered consciousness. All that could be made out was a ceaseless cry for "gingerbread nuts." Papa bought the poor fellow some pounds of these, but all they got from him was "gingerbread nuts," and so he died.

* * *

It was in the strong, bracing air of the country that I reveled until the obligations of my position necessitated my return to London. Lord Endover had gone to Scotland where he had taken a moor. I had decided not to accompany him. The weather had turned cold and wet. A week's visit to my old home would be enjoyable. Papa received me with a transport of delight.

"My darling Papa is always in the thoughts of his little girl."

"My sweet Eveline! You are more beautiful than ever! You have become rounder and fuller in your figure. The country air has been most beneficial to you. I have had no news from you recently of a private nature. Tell me, darling, has Lord Endover any hopes that . . . "

"I know all you would say, dear Papa. He has none, nor do I desire he should have. It is never likely to be as you suggest."

"I am not surprised, my dear Eveline. It is then as I thought."

"I am determined, Papa, never to perpetuate the race of Endovers. It is bad blood. If ever I had a child, a son, my offspring should have a father capable of procreating a new and healthy race which should endure—otherwise I am content to remain as I am."

He took me in his arms, mingling our kisses in tender sighs of ineffable enjoyment.

"Oh, my darling Eveline, what pleasure you give me!"

"My sweet Papa, you drown me in ecstasy. I am yours . . . yours only! What sweet adultery!"

"Oh Eveline, my child . . . incest is sweeter still."

In lascivious whispers we expanded the ideas which served to whet our ardent passion. Monstrous perceptions of enjoyment floated through our minds. They added poignancy to our lusty fuel to the fire of our already heated temperaments. We paused in our fierce and ravenous enjoyment. We lingered even as the epicure delights to taste to the full of a sumptuous repast, that we might enjoy each separate sensation. We worked ourselves almost to the point of consummation. Then we broke off only to recommence. I excited my darling Papa with every lewd suggestion my prurient imagination could devise. He made such proposals

73

under his breath that only demons of lust could have prompted. We were both drunk with desire, overwhelmed with the intoxication of this renewal of our intimacy.

I made no secret now of my discovery of his peephole. I went further; I asked him if he had enjoyed the exhibition, whether it had kindled his lust. Yes, and whether he would like me to act the scene over again—or another—a more obscene and outrageous one, in which there should be three actors.

In this way we laid our schemes. Thus we invented plans of voluptuous gratification which we determined mutually to carry out. In the midst of our transports, while our imaginations ran riot in a red whirl of Satanic excitement, we rushed together in the final spasmodic struggle. With a volley of erotic expletives, Papa drove his swollen limb and flooded me with a volume of his seed. Exhaustion followed nature's overwrought efforts. A sweet languor followed by a refreshing slumber in each other's arms restored the vigor we had so recently expended. Our fixed determination alone remained. We would indulge our voluptuous inclinations in the future as we had already proposed. We had invented a new pleasure, a lewd distraction of no ordinary kind.

* * *

Lord Endover came up to town. It had, no doubt, strong inducements for him. I knew him too well to suppose he would be firm enough to free himself entirely from the early allurements that fast life had woven around him.

All I feared was some lasting taint, some loathsome encounter which might entail ruin upon myself as well as my husband.

He would return home very late, or very early, rather, in the morning, from the club, of course. Always the club! If not this club, then that club. It was necessary that he should show himself in the House of Lords also. I grew quite accustomed to these excuses. I received them all with the imperturbable good humor of common sense. I only ventured to remark that I thought he worked too hard for an ungrateful country, but I took care to provide myself with a separate room; one that suited me well in every respect and communicated with a boudoir beyond.

There is no more ill-treated an institution than a man's club in London. The poor thing has to stand all the responsibility and receive all the vituperation of that large section of Society women who suffer from the husband who returns with the milk in the early morning. It is certainly remarkable how many of them believe, or pretend to believe, in the power of that select circle of men of good standing, which spreads its blandishments in the form of whist, cigars and brandies and sodas to the extinction of all natural desire to seek the warm and genuine embrace of the loving and still fresh wife at home.

The awakening comes soon and with it, in too many cases, the natural impulse of revenge by an angry woman surrounded by temptations, to carry her charms to a more profitable, if not more congenial market.

Lord L—— was naturally a frequent visitor.

I drove him in the park. He took me too, on several occasions, to the opera. When the opera season was over we visited the theaters. My husband was rarely at the party and Percy was quartered at Scotland.

*   *   *

"Tonight, Eveline, in accordance with your wish, I have arranged our little diversion. We start precisely at nine. You are still determined on the adventure?"

"I am ready, dear Papa. Indeed I long for the fun. We will do all we talked of and you will, I hope, be near. You will look on and enjoy it too, will you not? Oh, it will be delicious, if only I know you enjoy it through me."

We drove to our quiet street. I wore a veil. Lord L—— was also unrecognizable. He took me from the cab and we walked a short distance. We were absolutely alone. We turned a corner and stood at the door of the same house. He turned a handle and we passed in. A tall, fair young woman received us in the hall as if by appointment.

"The young men are here. Will you walk upstairs, please?"

I heard all she whispered to Papa.

"They quite understand everything; the lady will be pleased with them. I know they will amuse her. They are only too glad of the chance."

We followed the loquacious woman upstairs. She ushered us into the same room. The two carved brackets were in their places. On them stood the somewhat meaningless Chinese vases as on my last visit. Papa made haste to disappear. Presently the door opened again. Two young men entered. They closed the door and we three were left alone.

My first inclination was to laugh. We must have all looked a little awkward. They were fine, handsome young fellows, stout and broad shouldered, with what Lord L—— would have called plenty of "grit" in them. They were evidently well-to-do. Just the sort of men Eveline would love to enjoy. They promised well. She would not be balked of her pleasure nor, to judge by their look of pleased excitement, were they in any danger of being disappointed. A few words and we were soon on a social footing. They never took their eyes off my person. I sat on the sofa. They came uninvited and sat by me.

"You are not afraid of me, are you? You can be quite at your ease. You both know what a young woman is, don't you?"

"Yes, of course we do. Don't we, Tom? But we don't often see one like you. You're a beauty, a perfect one."

"She's a lovely bit, Bill, she's . . . oh my! I can't say any more. I'm longing for it already."

"How nice you both look. What are you longing for? Give me a kiss."

They vied with each other in snatching kisses from my hands, much and many from my lips and cheeks. I let them pull me this way and that as they wished. I shut my eyes. I let my imagination wander. My attention was quickly called back. One young fellow had insinuated his hand under my clothes. His com-

77

panion was kissing me on the mouth. I laid a hand on each side of me. I encountered their thighs. I had no difficulty in discovering the position of their privates. Both were already violently erect. They moved excitedly under my touches, which I made pointedly indecent. My right neighbor put his arm around me. He pulled me towards him and I kissed him on the lips. The other man put his left hand on the top of my bosom. I kissed him also.

"Let us be at our ease. Take off your coats; take off everything that is in the way. I want to see you as you are."

They rose quickly. In an incredibly short time they stood before me stripped to their shirts. Their trousers were flung into a chair.

My spirits rose. I was consumed with longing for the game to begin.

I raised their shirts as they stood before me. I grasped their stiff hairy members in my little hands. I determined to be as plainly lewd as possible. I was well aware I was overheard. I desired to make rich amends to the listener for his sacrifice. I knew he would appreciate every indecency, every salacious incident.

"What sweet pricks you have!"

They were in reality splendid, fine specimens of vigorous manhood. Their members confronted me menacingly as I commenced to finger them in turn. I bent down my head. I tickled and kissed them. I played around the soft warm things with my hot tongue. Both became furiously excited. They assisted me to undress. I slipped off my skirts and my bodice. I then stood in my chemise and stockings, retaining my pretty kid boots. Then I threw off my corset and gave them my warm body with which to play.

"What a lovely girl you are! I am longing to get into you."

"See, Tom, what a bottom she's got? Isn't she awfully well-made?"

They felt me all over. Tom went down on his knees. He divided my legs. He kissed my thighs all over. Then he pressed his face forward. He tried hard to arrive at my orbit. I put my hand down and shielded it. Resistance made him more eager.

"We both must have you, my dear. How would you like us to do it?"

"Say, which of us will have you first. I'm sure you're a dandy one when you've got a man up your sweet little belly."

I delighted in their rough indecencies. I knew someone else would also be enjoying them, someone of whose proximity my companions were both ignorant.

"Will you lie on your back, my fine girl? On the sofa first and let me put it into you?"

I pretended to become a little frightened.

"I don't know. I'm sure your things are both so dreadfully large and stiff."

In another second I was on my back on the sofa. It was exactly opposite the china vase to the left of the door. I gave a despairing look in that direction as the young fellow called Tom bent over me. He inserted his knees between my thighs while the other, with the greatest good humor, arranged a soft pillow for my head. Tom lay prone on my belly, his hairy chest pressing my soft breasts. My parts

79

were in no condition to resist him, potent as was this monstrous rammer. I was actually swimming in the moist exudation which kindly Nature produces in such an emergency. Already I felt the broad head of his instrument thrusting itself within my slit. With steady pressure he continued to penetrate.

"Put your hand under her bottom, Bill, I'm held in already. She's . . . she's . . . oh, she's awfully nice!"

"Make haste and give it to her. I want my turn."

Tom began a gentle undulation, supporting himself principally on his knees and hands. He raised his head. He looked into my face.

"Oh, my, you're into me! Oh, ah! Pray go gently. You're so strong. You're too bad!"

Bill's broad palm was still under my buttocks, which he raised up in unison with his friend's movements.

"Is that nice now, eh? Is he stroking you nicely? Hasn't he got a fine tool?"

It was impossible to answer. I stretched out my right arm. My hand encountered Bill's stiff weapon, only waiting the other's vacation of my parts to be itself inserted in the same place. I gasped with pleasure. Meanwhile, the act was proceeding with utmost vigor. The young fellow was in up to his balls. His rough belly, covered with an awfully black growth of curly hair, rubbed upon my satin skin with an exquisite sensation of lustful friction. I felt his limb vibrating with the delightful thrusts with which he was laboring my poor body.

"I've got my finger on the line between his

80

balls. I think he'll spend directly. You'll get a lot."

"Oh, Bill! He's up to my womb now."

Here were two men assisting in a single act. It was a new sensation. I found it delicious. My flexible parts were stretched around the stiff instrument like a glove. The other's finger seemed to act as a spur upon the other's genitals. He drove up and down furiously. He worked away with incredible energy. I felt the short spasmodic thrusts which precede the discharge. I came. He lay on me, pouring out his rapture. His sperm came from him, wetting my longing parts in rapid jets. When all was done he withdrew with reluctance, but urged thereto by his friend. Before I could even rise Bill sprang upon me. He got between my legs. He contemplated my naked body, red from the rough contact of his companion, as a hawk might gloat over its tender quarry. He lay down to his work, stretching my thighs open to receive his loins between. He pointed his strong limb to my body and my already reeking slit. He drove it into me until I felt the crisp hairs on his belly chafing my mount.

It was a new sensation for me. I found it exquisite. The heat, the slippery condition I was in, the knowledge that the young fellow would spend and thereby double the flood I had already received, wound up my imagination to fever heat.

The big member of my second ravisher seemed to swell to an enormous extent, caused probably by the fervent temperature of my own parts. He seemed very long in bringing

81

the lewd business to a climax, though his limb hardened until it resembled a truncheon of wood. He worked away with frenzy. At length I felt him spend. He spouted a second emission into me. He was so long in doing it I thought he would never finish. At last the final drops were exuded. The human cascade had run dry. My chemise was saturated with their sperm. Even the holland cover on the sofa was marked with a big wet patch. I rose hastily. I made my toilet behind the screen which covered the position of the necessary furniture. We all three then reposed on the sofa pressed together like sardines in a box. Each of my new friends vied with the other in their indecencies and their suggestions.

How I passed the entire hour during the time which these two fine young men kept me wantonly at their service, it is impossible to record. I only know I experienced a round of voluptuous enjoyment indulged amid smothered cries of intense nervous exultation. At last I believe I slept.

I recollect a quaint triangular adieu and a long silence. Then the voice of Lord L—— sounded in my ears and I threw my arms around Papa's neck. He had been a witness to all that had passed. He explained the secret of the little cabinet. He showed me the interior. I looked out at the opening. It could be effectually closed with a wine cork. There were two of these peepholes arranged for seeing and speaking through. Securely screened among the carved foliage of the bracket and immediately under the shelf on which stood the large china vase, no one would suspect their presence, which was rendered doubly unlikely by the blackened corks when not in use. The partition between the two rooms was only a thin paneling of wood.

"I should like to be with you, dear Papa, and share your curious pleasure by witnessing someone else. Could we not see someone on another occasion, just as today you have seen us?"

"I have no doubt it could be managed. I will make inquiries. Money, my dear, will buy anything in London."

"No, Papa dear. No money could buy off the love—the wicked, willful, ardent love that Eveline holds for you."

"Well spoken, my darling. However, it will serve our purpose in this matter. Next week, if you have time and an opportunity, we may bring off an exhibition of a peculiarly interesting character."

CHAPTER 5

How sweet is the country air. How lovely the blue water of the lake which sparkles in the sunlight beneath the shadows of the trees. Yet winter is upon us—winter in Cumberland. I have no taste to remain and encounter the snow and the cold. Chitterlings is delightful in the summer. It is not altogether such a residence as I would choose for the winter months. Endover is still away in the North shooting. I feel also much inclined for a little sport, though I fancy I would be on more congenial ground were I to be shot at and become a target of some gallant gun.

I reached the great gate which gave entrance to the avenue. Mrs. Hodge, the gatekeeper's wife, ran out all wreathed in smiles to open it, a buxom, good looking woman of some seven or eight and 20 years of age. After her came toddling a chubby lad of some three summers. A second held on by the lodge post, just getting firm on his legs.

I looked on, well-pleased to pause in my solitary walk to regale my sight with the picture so rural, so natural, so unobtainable. No; money cannot purchase all. There are gifts for which Nature refuses such dross; blessings which are sometimes unobtainable for all that wealth may have to offer.

"Good morning, Mrs. Hodge. Why, bless me, what fine boys. Are they both your own?"

"Well, yes, My Lady. They are mine—and my man's too. This is my eldest. Yonder one's my second. That's all, My Lady. All at present."

"Ah, Mrs. Hodge, you are a lucky woman to have such splendid children. They are perfect."

"I don't know about that, My Lady, but this one's christened Christopher. The parson gave us the name of a merchant captain who sailed over to America. Christopher Columbus his whole name was. That's Columbus standing by the door. He's just a year old last week, My Lady, and can walk and run till it's all I can do to catch him. But Lord bless him! He's a good little lad."

"I quite envy you. I fear such happiness is not for all the world. Have you a good husband, Mrs. Hodge?"

"Lord bless you, My Lady, that I have. My Jock is never so happy as when his work's done and we sit inside together of an evening. He reads a lot then, all aloud to me, for you see, My Lady, he works hard in the woods, cutting timber all day on the estate out yonder, and he takes his supper hearty, he does, and then he sits and smokes and reads."

"How long have you been married, **Mrs. Hodges?**"

"Nigh on to four years, now, My Lady."

"You've not lost any time, I see."

I laughed. The good woman joined my merriment.

"Lord, Ma'am—Your Ladyship, I mean—I beg pardon—if you only knew how rampageous my Jock gets! Why, I had all the trouble in my life to keep him decently quiet when we were courting, and since we've married there's no holding him. He's like a mad horse, he is."

"And what age is your husband, Mrs. Hodge?"

"Jock's nigh on a year younger than me, My Lady."

"Younger, is he! That is rather unusual in these parts is it not?"

"I don't know, My Lady, but saving your presence, his parents were both dead and gone. He had no home. I had saved up a bit of money here in the dairy and so they gave me the chance at the lodge if we chose to marry and look after each other."

"You're a happy woman, Mrs. Hodge?"

Something in my voice seemed to raise all the woman's tender sympathy. She looked at me inquiringly.

"I hope, My Lady, you won't think me too bold, but we've all of us on the estate been hoping as how My Lord might have an heir."

I pretended not to understand.

"I always thought hares were unusually plentiful this time about Chitterlings.

Mrs. Hodge looked nonplussed.

86

"I don't mean hares what run, but heirs."

"Oh, I see! Yes, now I see. It is very kind of you, I'm sure. At present, Mrs. Hodge, we must be content as we are."

The good woman drew closer. There was an air of mystery in her open, honest, good face, a look almost of trouble. She shook her head as she slowly uttered her next remark.

"I shouldn't. No, there's something wrong somewhere. Saving your presence, My Lady, and Your Ladyship'll excuse me, but a lovely beautiful well-grown young lady like Your Ladyship has no call to be childless. You may send me off for my impudence or turn us out of the lodge, but after being brought up on the estate, and it's now nigh on 29 years ago I was born on it, I do say now, Your Ladyship ought to have an heir."

There was something in Mrs. Hodge's kindly meant comments which touched me. There was even a dimness in her eyes as her broad, good-humored face looked into mine.

"No, I shouldn't be content. I know there's a difference in the living and the ways of great people and the like of us poor folks, but if I were the Lady of the manor without an heir, I know all the village would want to know why. I can keep my mouth shut, My Lady. I'm not a woman to go about gossiping about what don't concern me. I keeps to myself; but if Your Ladyship heard all they said you would find they knew it wasn't your fault."

The woman looked so kindly sympathetic that I suppressed a natural inclination to re-

87

sentment. It rose in my throat. What! The Countess of Endover, Lady of the Manor of Chitterlings in my own right, to be thus spoken to and pittied by a peasant on my own estate! No, but it would not do. I broke down. The position was too strained. The tears rose to my eyes. Mrs. Hodge saw my distress. The kindly woman's own sweet nature came up beaming in her sympathetic look as she took my hand and kissed it.

"I know, I know, My Lady. My Lord takes his shooting—takes his hunting. He can do a long day in the covers perhaps, but he's—he's not to be compared to us poor folks under the sheets."

"What do you mean, Mrs. Hodge? My husband, Lord Endover, is all that is kind, all that is . . ."

"Ah, no, My Lady, you must excuse me—I mean no wrong. I only talk as I feel for Your Ladyship. It's not your fault. It's his."

I withdrew my hand. An angry light must have shown in my eyes. My red blood flew to my cheek. I drew myself up. This woman's insolence should not go unpunished. I was mad enough to have been accosted in this style, but to be an object of downright pity—no, this was too much.

"You are angry, My Lady—and no wonder! I am only a poor ignorant woman. You are a great lady. I hope you will forgive me. I meant all right for the best. I could tell you more . . ."

I hesitated. There was an air of reality about the elderly woman I could not mistake.

"Come in here, My Lady. I will explain all. I will tell you all I have to tell. The Lord knows I have no reason to hide it. It's too well-known already."

I entered the comfortable dwelling. Mrs. Hodge carefully dusted a chair with her apron. I sat down and she dropped on both knees in front of me, holding her bony face in her hands. Suddenly she looked up. Her confidence seemed to return. Her cheeks were wet with tears, red and mottled.

"I want to tell you all about it. I always said to myself I would. It was not all my fault. He was old enough to have known better than to take advantage of a poor girl without experience. He was educated and rich, with ladies all around for his asking. I was taken in with his winning ways. I was foolishly proud of his noticing me. He did what he liked with me. More's the pity. He said it was all a bit of fun and nonsense and that he would take care of me. Father came to hear of it. Mother was dead then. The village all heard of it. They sneered at father. It broke his heart. He beat me and turned me out of doors. An old neighbor took me in out of charity like. It killed father. I was left alone. The Countess was kind to me. The last dowager, I mean. She's dead now, and he—can you guess who he was? Yes, I know you do, My Lady."

Down went her head again between her hands. I heard a low sobbing moan. Then she spoke again.

"Fortunately nothing came of my wrongdoing. I lived it down. Then Jock came my way.

He was always a good lad. A bit studious like. Clever at farm work, strong and cheery. I took to him. We married. The dowager Lady Endover had directed them to take care of me. They gave us the lodge. Jock is keeper, as Your Ladyship knows."

Mrs. Hodge looked all around. Seeing that we were quite alone but for the two children playing on the floor, she went on.

"It was then I knew why nothing had come of my wrongdoing. He was not like my Jock. He had not the way of doing what men who take up with young girls ought—I mean are expected—to do. He was weak. Almost without any force at all after the novelty of Jock. It was different with my Jock, my goodness, yes, My Lady. Why I couldn't hold him. He was like a cage filled with lions under the blankets. There wasn't no stopping him. Under ten months my baby was born. My second was planted the first time ever he touched me after I was through with the suckling of the first. And, My Lady, I don't mind telling you my third is coming the same."

Mrs. Hodge rose to her feet. She was quite dramatic in her excitement. As she unfolded her narrative the truth had gradually come to me. It was the old story—like a penny novel. But there was more to it than that. This view struck me also. Every word was obviously true. She had told me at least one fact I recognized only too well. Very naturally she had fallen into an error in her knowledge of only half the facts. Very possibly, as regards my matrimonial affairs, there existed a DOUBLE disqualification. I felt angry at having been deceived. I had been married only a year. I felt I was looked upon all around as a failure —a disappointment. In a flash it suddenly occurred to me why the three sisters of the Earl had commenced a course of subservient patronage towards their cousin, the heir apparent to the title. It was even said the youngest was going to marry him. Many things hitherto hidden from my understanding now became clear. If the cousin, a worthless, idle creature obtained the title, Chitterlings would one day be hers. My woman's instincts were aroused.

"Go on, Mrs. Hodge, I am much interested. Alas! I think it is much as you say. But still I fear there is nothing to be done. I must be content to be as I am. You are blessed with two beautiful children, boys fit to be kings. You have a fine young fellow for a husband, replete with health and strength, while I . . ."

The good woman dropped to her knees again. She came closer and gazed into my face with a puzzled look I could not decipher.

"I shouldn't My Lady. No, not in your place —I shouldn't! It ain't in Nature. What! Let all go to nobody knows where! A fine title! A fine estate! When all might be for you and yours but for the fault of a certain person who has passed his time in ruining his faculties. Look on my boys there. My Jock's the man that knows the trick. Oh, my dear Lady, try my Jock!"

Mrs. Hodge clasped my hand, took it between her own and slobbered kisses on it.

*　　*　　*

91

"What, my darling Eveline, you are in town again! So unexpected, too. I thought you had intended remaining at Chitterlings sometime longer."

"So I did, dear Papa, but I have changed my mind. Ladies are apt to be fickle you know."

"But you are not fickle, my dear. You stick to your old love, my sweet little girl. Or your little hand would not be in mine now."

"Do you like to feel your little Eveline's hand right *there* Papa? Is it nice? Does it make you feel you love your own little girl? Do you still like my kisses? Do they give you pleasure? Is my tongue warm and soft? Is it all that which makes this sweet thing so stiff and long? Let me caress it, dear Papa."

"Oh, my God! Eveline! You kill me with pleasure. Your tongue and lips are maddening me. Take care or I shall fill your mouth!"

"Well, Papa, and what then? Do I not love your sweet sperm?"

"Oh, stay! You drive me mad. Not again! Oh? It is in your mouth. You are rolling your hot tongue round the nut. Oh, there, there! Take all—all!"

"You and I shall sleep together tonight, dear Papa, shall we not? You will make the bed go crickey-crack when you are on top of your own little girl, will you not?"

"There is a ball at Lady A——'s in Eaton Square. You had an invitation, I know. It is for the day after tomorrow. Will you go, Eveline? A dance will do you good. If you say yes, I will take you myself."

"Then I will go, dear Papa. Endover is

coming to London. I have sent for him from the North."

"What can be the matter, my darling? I hope nothing is wrong."

"Nothing is wrong in the ordinary sense, but I have come to a decision. I am not satisfied with the state of my health; not altogether sure that things might not be set right as regards my—my present condition, Papa."

"Eveline, you alarm me. One would fear you are not well."

"I am quite well—and quite resolved. One thing is certain: I have been married over 12 months. Endover is becoming more morose. He has given up, domestically. He goes here and there. He writes after every weary interval we pass together, if I have any news for him. I understand what he means."

"My poor darling!"

"You remember our conversation, Papa? Who knows what may be the cause of my sterility? For such it is. I have decided to consult a London physician. I have sent for my husband to hear his opinion after a proper examination. I should like you to be with him on the occasion, dear Papa."

"I think you are very wise. The stake is an enormously important one. It is worth playing for. I will not disguise from you that the Earl has already lamented the loss of all his hopes, in my hearing."

"We shall see. At any rate I will not leave this chance untried."

*   *   *

"Are you ready, Eveline? The carriage is at the door. Although you will not want for partners I should not in your place be late. The supper is arranged, they tell me, for an unusually early hour. Lady A—— likes her guests to dance, as sailors say, with the champagne all aboard."

"How dreadful, dear Papa. I want no such stimulant. I have not danced since my marriage. You must give me a square dance."

"Never mind, as Percy would say, let's make a night of it. But I must leave you early. I have an important engagement to meet the new Viceroy at the Club."

"Yes, I mean to make a night of it, Papa. I may not have such a chance again. But come and take me home."

Papa laughed. I could see that my humor made him nervous. He changed the subject.

"How superbly beautiful you look, my dear child. How lovely your dress, and yet so simple. It does not look good enough for the Countess of Endover, though. But still it is very becoming. What gloves! Your long white gloves are absolutely ravishing. They look so infinitely delicate and soft. They fit like the skin they are, but then, your darling hand is perfect. Your bracelets, too, are selected with perfect taste, so simple and yet so chaste."

"Let us go then, dear Papa. You kill me with your kind hearted flattery. Endover cares nothing now for all the points you mention."

The dancing had been in full swing for some time when we arrived. I found a chance to give Papa a quadrille. Several young men were introduced to me. I selected one—an old acquaintance. We waltzed together. He danced well. The music was good, the time perfect. I thoroughly enjoyed myself. The strains of the melody died away. The dancers stopped. Supper was announced. My partner thought himself the happiest of men to lead me downstairs to partake of it. I was thirsty. The champagne was grateful to my feverish palate. I left the table at the first opportunity. I wanted air. My head ached. I found myself in the entrance hall. The house door was open. An awning had been erected down to the curb. A solitary footman stood in attendance just below the steps. The night breeze was refreshing. I looked behind; I was alone. I advanced a step or two beyond the doorway. I drew the hood of my opera cloak over my head.

"Looking for a carriage, Miss? Shall I find it for you?"

"Oh, no. Thank you very much. It is not here. I felt faint. I want to breathe the fresh air. It is so fine a night. The heat inside is oppressive."

"Yes, Miss. A lovely night. Would you like a quiet turn around in the carriage? Do you good."

I took a rapid survey of the man. He was of the ordinary type; tall, good-looking to a certain extent, and wearing a livery which I did not recognize. It was evident that he knew me.

I flashed such a glance at him as I flatter myself Eveline knows how to give with effect. He caught its intensity.

"It would perhaps be nice. I suffer so, but . . . well, just take me around half of the square at a walk. I think it would do my head good.

The footman whistled. A large closed landau and pair came up out of the darkness. He held open the door. I swiftly stepped in. As I half suspected he would, the man followed. He closed the door, giving a quiet direction to the coachman as he did so. The footman sat himself opposite on the edge of the seat with his back to the horses.

"I still feel faint. My head aches badly—the heat of the room was dreadful."

My self-imposed companion promptly whipped out a fan from the pocket behind him. He began agitating it gently before my face as I reclined on the comfortable cushions. The horses were going at a walk. The night was moonless. The gas lamps alone shone an uncertain streak of light into the carriage at intervals as we passed. By their aid I furtively summed up my neighbor. He was evidently much agitated. His whole bearing betrayed an eagerness hardly compatible with his innocent employment. He bent forward in order to fan me. The better to steady himself, he rested his left hand on my knee. He pushed one of his sturdy legs between my knees. I felt his calf against mine. I was exhaled from myself in the close atmosphere. He evidently inhaled it. It seemed to madden him.

"There, you're better now, Miss. It'll soon pass off."

I could see that his eyes were intent on my face which had emerged from my hood. He stole fervent glances at my bosom, also particularly on the gloved and delicate hands with the left of which I held my cloak not too tightly closed. The right pressed my lace kerchief to my lips. An irrepressible feeling of the absurdity of the situation possessed me. I had difficulty restraining my inclination to laugh. He advanced his left hand a little farther. He even pressed closer with his fingers. He moved his leg at the same time more boldly between mine.

"Oh, you must not do that. You are shockingly indelicate."

There was only coquetry in my voice; only an invitation in my glance. The man noted both. He grew bolder still. I felt quite as wanton as he. My position was exceedingly critical.

"I think you have fanned me enough, thank you. It makes me rather cold. Oh, pray, pray do not put your hand there."

He closed the fan. It fell between us. In stooping to pick it up his hand touched my ankle. Instantly I felt it slip up to my calf. Just then we crossed the lamplight. I saw his face all flushed, his lips apart, his eyes dilated with strong sensual craving. There was no stopping him now. I could stand it no longer. I tittered.

"Oh, don't, pray don't! You must not do that."

His hot hand advanced. He touched my knee. His left hand was under my clothes still. I put down my own in a well-feigned effort to stop him. He seized it with his. He caressed it softly. He fondled the well gloved fingers. He stroked the perfumed kid on my wrist and arm. Suddenly he drew my hand towards his.

He pressed it down on his person. He was fairly aflame with passion. My hand, retained in his strong grasp, detected his condition. Within his garment I felt his limb. It was evidently a fine long one—stiff as buckram and very thick. The contact excited me further.

"How delicious you are! Don't take your lovely little hand away."

A gentle squeeze was all my response. He took care I should not leave off my inspection. It fired my blood. He slightly jerked his loins. I bent my body nearer his own. I repeated the squeeze even more suggestively. He pressed and squeezed my hand on his person.

"Do you feel so naughty then? Let me look at it."

He released his grasp. He quickly unbuttoned his trousers. He pulled up his shirt. A big red-topped member started out. Oh, how long it was and how dreadfully stiff! Curving slightly upward, the swollen head was already naked and staring me in the face. I put my gloved hand upon it. I took it in my palm. My right hand covered the protruding knob. I shook it. He could hardly retain his seat. He thrust his eager fingers into the front of my low dress.

"What shall I do with this? What a large one you have!"

I pressed back with both my hands. He tried to raise my dress. I stopped him.

"Oh, no, it is impossible. You would rumple my dress. You must be very gentle. Sit still —Oh, do, pray!"

I love to finger a man's limb when it is of

98

such splendid proportions. This man's was excellently molded. It stood awaiting my inspection. There was no reserve between us now. Modesty had flown out the window. We understood each other.

"But what can we do? Pray let me put it into you. I won't hurt you. I'll be as gentle as a lamb. I won't tumble your clothes. It won't take a minute. The coachman is a 'fly' — no one will know. Let me pass my hand up. Let me feel all you have got."

"Ah, no, no! It won't do! I must go back. What do you think they would say of me if they saw me enter all tumbled and rumpled? Sit still—sit still! Is that nice?"

I moved both my hands gently up and down on his huge limb. Each stroke covered and then exposed the red gland. He breathed heavily. He ceased his attack. He pushed his loins forward.

"Nice? Oh, yes! My God! It's delicious! You'll bring it on!"

"Bring it on? Do you mean that I should milk you? Is that so very nice? Like that? And so—like that? Do you like me to play with it?"

"Oh, yes! It's lovely—you'll milk me, Miss, won't you? Oh, oh! Do stop a little Miss."

The horses had stopped. The carriage appeared to be drawn up under the trees close to the square railings, in the dark place near the side. I bent my head lower. I examined the man's limb as well as I could by the uncertain light. It was a model of manly health and vigor. I stooped lower still. My wet and eager lips touched the purple lips below. How

99

soft they were. How delicious the masculine flavor. I kissed them repeatedly. A second later it slipped into my mouth. The man seemed to resign himself. He sighed with delight. My tongue was thrust below the velvet plumlike nut. He pushed the head and shoulders quite into my gullet. I sucked all I could. My gloved hands tickled and pressed the long shaft. He commenced to wriggle on the edge of the back seat. He held his legs straightened wide apart. He threw back his head.

"Oh, my God! Stop . . . no . . . go . . . on!"

I obeyed. He thrust forward. I received a mouthful. He spent furiously. I held on. I caught it all to the last drop. I was half-mad with erotic pleasure. He groaned aloud in his spasmodic discharge as I drew spendings from him. I wiped my lips with my lace handkerchief. He sat up and rearranged his clothes. We listened; then my companion cautiously opened the door. He got out and I heard another voice. The door was closed but the window was on the last button.

"What have you got inside, Chris?"

"Oh, don't ask—a regular stunner. It's a young lady from the ball at No.——. She's all right—she—oh my! I can't speak yet, I've just done it. I've had such a time!"

"Well get out of the way. Keep a lookout for the sergeant. He won't be back along this way just yet."

The door opened again. A strong light was flashed in my face.

"What's up here? What's up?"

The carriage opened wider. A policeman thrust himself in and sat on the front seat.

100

"I don't know that I oughtn't to run you in, Miss (they all called me Miss) there's been a fine goings-on here. Well, I never! A handsome, beautiful young girl like you. What have you two been doing of? I think I know. He's a nice chap is Chris, but he's clumsy, that's what he is. I should like a go at it myself. Give me a kiss, my beauty. There, don't be shy. It's only my way, you know."

"Oh, please, you mustn't put your hands there. You hurt, you are so rough. You will tear my dress. Let me alone. I say! Oh! pray don't . . . don't do that."

"Sit quiet. I'm in with these chaps. Why they couldn't do nothing without me. It's on my beat you see Miss. Sit quiet, I won't hurt you. But I mean to have you like Chris did."

All this time he was pulling me about with his right hand. He was engaged in unbuttoning his clothes with the other. He had no shame. He pulled out a long white member. He shook it at me impudently in the uncertain light. He was a tall, strong man.

"Now, Miss, just keep quiet or I shall have to do my duty."

"Oh, my goodness, policeman, how dreadfully naughty you are. But, oh dear! What shall I do? Tell me, are you a married man?"

"Yes, I am that. I've a missus at home and three kids. But she ain't a patch to you. You're just to my liking. A real beauty. But what do you want to ask me that for?"

"Well . . . I don't know . . . but if you really are married, and if you are very, very gentle . . ."

101

"Oh, shut up! I can't wait! Here, turn up your skirt. I want to see your legs."

The wretch put down his hands. He begged me to help him. I did all I could to save the dress. He saw my stockings up to the knees. His truncheon was stiff enough in all conscience now. I saw it plainly sticking up in a wild erection. He pulled me forward to the edge of the seat. He slipped on his knees. He had showed me one of his hands up my clothes. His other arm was around my loins pulling me towards him. His eager fingers were already in contact with my private parts. Secretly I enjoyed his rough toying. My skirts were now up until he could see my white belly. He rudely pushed my thighs asunder.

"Oh, Christ! What a fine little bit you are! You make me awfully randy. Here, take this in your hand. Come! No nonsense now! I can't wait, I tell you! Put it in yourself!"

He forced me to take his truncheon in my gloved hand. I squeezed it. It was level with the place he sought. He thrust forward. I let it slip in. He no sooner felt the hot contact than he pushed it up into me, dragging me close to him. He thrust it in up to the balls. He began to move.

"Now, I'll do the business for you. How do you like that, My Lady?"

"Oh, policeman, how you do push!"

The man worked violently up and down my vagina. He was too excited to be long over the job. He seized me in a vise. Almost immediately I felt him spending. I went off also. I was in the agony of sensuous delight. His sperm was thick and hot. He waited a moment to recover his breath. He drew his limb out and got up. As he did so I noticed a face against the window. It was the footman. He opened the door.

"Come out. I know you've had the young lady. I saw you through the glass. I'm awful randy now. There's time yet. There's no one about. Look out a minute while I have a go."

He entered the carriage and closed the door. He let loose a huge member. It seemed stiffer and bigger than before.

"Now, Miss, I can't help it. He had you and so will I."

"Oh, you beast, what are you doing! Let me alone! Don't thrust my legs open. You'll kill me! What a size it is! Why . . . you're right into me!"

He had already penetrated. He forced the huge thing into me until he seemed to be right up to my womb. He uttered no words. He only breathed hard. And pushed up in his strong excitement. Then his head fell on my shoulder. I knew he was spending. He emitted in short spasmodic jerks. Like his friend, he made haste to escape.

Before he could close the door I heard the flick of the whip. And then a new and very gruff voice said:

"Here, I say! What the hell are you fellows about? I'm going to get down. The old box is shaking about so awful I can't hold the bloody horses."

Just then I heard a scramble. The policeman rushed across the road. The footman got turned rapidly about and then went slowly

103

back toward No.———. I adjusted myself as best I could. I pulled my large opera cloak over my head and was set down once more. I passed hastily in and gained the ladies' retiring room. There I found myself alone. The wild strains of a lovely waltz were filling the air. I took care to repair the damage and changed my gloves.

"Oh, my dear Eveline, I have been looking for you."

"Poor Papa. I had a headache. But it is better now. Have you been making a night of it? I have enjoyed myself thoroughly. Take me home now. I have danced enough."

* * *

Doctor Brookstead-Hoare was a dapper little man. He came of a medical family. His father had commenced life as an assistant to an apothecary and subsequently practiced as such himself. The doctor's brown curly hair, already tinged with gray, was crisply combed around his small and shapely head. His finely-cut features presented nothing in their repose which betrayed his exalted opinion of his own powers, or person. When he spoke, however, his animation increased noticeably.

His mode of expression was adapted to the circumstance of the case. He was obsequiousness itself to the wealthy and the noble; short and terribly decisive to the meek and lowly. He emphasized his opinion with a sort of professional superiority which contrasted with the quaintly careless garrulity of his ordinary conversation. His self-conceit was enormous, and although a valuable adjuntcy in his pose before his patients, it raised a sort of hilarious resentment among his professional confreres, who saw through it.

Dr. Brookstead-Hoare possessed a large practice as a specialist for the treatment of women and children. He was altogether a professional pet of Society in his special department. His fees were immense, but only commensurate with his consummate complacency. He delighted to talk of the notabilities whom he counted among his patients. The pains and sufferings of royalty were all subservient to his skill. If his communications concerning them were not always correct, that at least served to extend his importance as a specialist.

"I have made a most careful examination in this case—ahem!—Her Ladyship—the Countess of Endover—yes, aided by my friend Dr. Archer, who is, I believe, your family adviser. A most thorough and careful examination. I find—ahem!—I find that there is no possible chance of Her Ladyship ever becoming a mother—ahem!—in her present condition. I have, however, ascertained quite beyond the possibility of a doubt, that a trifling . . . let us say . . . a very trivial operation would remove this . . . this disability. There is a small ligament which interferes with the proper position of the organs relatively, which interrupts the . . . the natural sequence of events. I cannot very well demonstrate this to the lay mind, but Doctor Archer and myself are in accord that it could be easily and safely removed. Our dear Countess is in every other way so beautifully and—ahem!—so perfectly

105

formed that I have no doubt, if she be willing to submit to this slight operation, she will have no cause thereafter to disappoint her Lord. Do I make myself clear? It is for Her Ladyship to decide."

Here the little man struck his hands together and placed them under the coattails as he balanced himself in front of the fire, reminding one strongly of a bantam cock contemplating crowing.

Our own family doctor looked anxiously towards me. My husband and Papa looked at one another in mute astonishment.

"The necessities of the case would, of course, entail a little sacrifice of time and comfort on the part of Her Ladyship. There would be the usual antiseptic and anesthetics to adminster, which Dr. Archer would undertake of course, and, then the slight operation to undergo—ahem!—let us say a week's rest and all would be in order again."

The Earl looked immensely relieved. He regarded me wistfully. Papa wore an expression of anxiety mingled with doubt. I put an end to the suspense.

"I am ready to undergo the operation as soon as the arrangements can be made. Tomorrow, if you will; the sooner the better. I have made up my mind. I will take my chance."

My husband actually shed tears of delight. He pressed my hand. The two doctors beamed graciously upon me. Papa hid his emotions behind a well-affected compliment to my courage. Dr. Brookstead-Hoare hastened to reply.

"Be it so—tomorrow at noon—ahem!—I will

be at your mansion. Oh, yes, I know the address. Leave all the arrangements to Dr. Archer. He will, I know, have all in readiness."

The little medico made an entry in his notebook. Then he pompously bowed us all out.

A vision of dissappointed sisters, of a cousin remitted to his pothouses and his scum of Society, flashed across my mind as I took my seat in the carriage, though none the easier for the disturbances caused by the exhaustive examination I had undergone.

*　　*　　*

I had now great reasons to be satisfied with the resolution I had formed. The earlier intimation I had received from my medical friend proved without doubt to be correct. The operation, I was informed by both physicians, had been perfectly successful.

"Dr. Archer says I may sit up today, Papa. And I may have what I like to eat."

"I have sent for oysters, my dear Eveline, and Mrs. Lockett will send you up a roast grouse, also a custard pudding of her own special make."

"How kind of you! Today I shall have fare like a queen; but oysters, you know, are supposed to stimulate other nerves than those of mere digestion."

"Yes, that is so. I believe I have felt the influence myself, especially when near my dear Eveline. No doubt they have a certain effect. Certain kinds of fish have the same result. The skate, that nutritious and much neglected fish, is one of them."

107

I could not help smiling at the serious professional air he assumed while thus lecturing. I let him see the twinkle in my eye.

"You mustn't eat oysters, and you mustn't eat skate, dear Papa, when you come near your little Eveline. She has a certain resolution and she intends to keep it."

He drew a face of such abject misery that I could not repress a little laugh at his expense.

"You are too cruel. Eveline, my child, but perhaps you act for the best. You will always have a will of your own which has hitherto led you to avoid pitfalls."

"I did not mean to be so terribly severe as altogether to exclude those delicacies from my dear Papa's diet . . . only that . . . only . . . you see, Papa . . . Well! We must be careful how we go about things now. At the same time, my great Charlemagne is a great conqueror. He cannot be expected to go altogether without the reward of his victories."

"I do not understand, my darling, quite what you mean."

"I will try to explain myself, dear Papa. When the Emperor Charlemagne first indulged in the luxury of a debauch with his daughters you may be sure he was not long in arriving at a complete enjoyment of their charms. Then came a time when the pleasures of dalliance succeeded to the hot lust of passionate desire. No doubt those recipients of the great man's favors were early taught those auxiliary delights which go to make up the full pleasure of sensual gratification. Do you follow me, dear Papa?"

108

He nodded, drew his chair closer to my bed and I saw my opportunity. I was not slow to take advantage of it. I only dreaded his terrible disappointment.

"We must be careful. I have fully determined there shall be a direct heir to the Earldom of Endover. I believe in myself. In so doing, I have already won half the battle. But I will have no weakling or ailing offspring of a race which has groveled in all the vices of the Georgian period, whose blood is as tainted as their morals are degenerate."

"My dear Eveline! Are you not a little hard on the Endovers?"

"Hard on them! If you only knew all I have learned concerning them! The men, I mean the father, grandfather—the progenitors of this noble, unadulterated family—why, had the grandfather of my husband not had the good fortune to have hit upon a French millionaire and married the pork-slaughterer's vulgar daughter, there would not have been an acre left, nor a hearth to warm the vapid blood of his son, let alone his grandson. No, Papa, and the estate, if I bear a child to succeed to the title, shall at least revert to one of sound, strong English blood. You may leave the rest to your little Eveline."

"My God, you are right, my child! I have unbounded confidence with you. But how will you compass all this? How carry out your idea?"

"As I have said before, dear Papa, leave it all to me. I believe I shall succeed in all. I have faith in myself—we shall see. I am going down to Chitterlings. Endover goes with

109

me. We are to have a second honeymoon, he says. There will be at least the horns of a new moon for him, and very little honey for me—the less the better."

"You frighten me, Eveline. I trust all will turn out as you hope."

I indulged in a little quiet laughter. I put forward my lips to be kissed. He bent over me; our lips met. For a second my tongue touched his. His eyes lighted up with passion.

"You must not let me change my position, dear Papa. Pull your chair closer yet . . . so, that will do."

I gently thrust my right hand from out of the bed. I had arranged a little diversion for him which I knew would exactly meet the exigencies of the case. My beautiful white kid glove covered my hand, and half my arm, fitting like my own skin. On my wrist sparkled a lovely diamond bracelet, his own gift. He looked down. He beheld the snakelike advance of the little gloved hand and the glistening sheen of the perfumed glove itself.

"Oh, Eveline, all that for me? How deliciously inviting is that beautiful little hand!"

He seized it, covered it with hot kisses.

"We must be careful, dear Papa, how we handle things now. Come, let me handle yours. Do you understand better now? Let me give my dear Papa all the pleasure my active little fingers can bestow. I am to remain still, but Dr. Archer says I may use my hands and arms. I want to avail myself of his kind permission. How stiff it is already! How delightful to feel its long white shaft. Oh, how I long to kiss it! But no! I want—I want to see your

110

sweet sperm come out. I want to bathe my new gloves in it. Let me have this pleasure, dear Papa!"

I knew him so well. I was quite aware of his peculiar lechery. I grasped the erected member. He leaned over me. I whispered the old indecencies in his ear—the old invitations in so many crude expressions. I bade him not to spare my nice new glove. He flushed; his lips grew dry and hot. The door was locked, no one had a right to disturb us. I slipped my nimble fingers up and down on his darling weapon. I squeezed it, I bore back the loose skin.

"Oh, my child! Oh! Ah! You give me an ecstasy of pleasure!"

"Is that nice, dear? You wicked Papa! You will spoil my beautiful glove! You will be coming directly—I know you will! You cannot help it—there! Do I rub this big thing as you like? Oh! see how red the top is now! What a contrast with the satin white of my glove! Oh, a little drop already! Quite a beautiful pearl! Oh Papa! there will be a quantity of it, will there not?"

He breathed hard and bore up toward me. He held back his clothes to avoid the consequences of his discharge. I had my handkerchief ready. His lovely member was rapidly manipulated by my hand. How I doted on the big, impudently obtrusive thing as I shook it up and down! His delight was evident. Enjoyment gave expression to his hard respiration, his open mouth, his upturned eyes. I knew by all the symptoms he was on the verge of his climax.

111

He arrived. He straightened himself. I grasped my victim firmly. He discharged. The hot, thick semen came slopping over my hand. My glove slipped about in the steaming flow. He pushed up towards me to meet my rapid movements until he had emitted the last drops. Then he sank back exhausted in his seat.

"Go at once and get a glass of wine, dear Papa. I must not have you reduced so much again for a long time to come."

* * *

There is no change so beneficial for a convalescent as the sweet country air of the lake district. The bracing breezes of Chitterlings would, I hoped, do much for me. Perhaps I expected their influence to be seconded by more potent agencies. The Earl was with me. Endover was in his gayest humor. The day had been a long and fatiguing one. I begged him to excuse me. I retired early. I told him I felt worn out and tired. He wished to join me in my chamber. I again begged him to excuse me, asking him to be reasonable because of my exhaustion. Tomorrow perhaps, yes, tomorrow night he should share my bed. My loving arms would celebrate our second honeymoon. They would reward him for all his forbearance. There would be no reason to complain of the coldness of his little wife.

I lay awake that night. I resolved in my mind about the many instances of the Earl's indifference; his utter neglect when first, after so brief a period, he had treated me as he had so many other women before me when the novelty of possession had worn off. I felt a disgust, a loathing for him I could not shake off. I thought of his low amours, of all I had heard, of those I knew only too well were his present companions. I remembered the pitiful history which poor Mrs. Hodge had revealed. As I did so, a thought came to my mind of her tearful, honest face. Did she contemplate a secret and terrible retribution? Was she capable in her apparent simplicity of such a double scheme? I would know more tomorrow. I would satisfy myself ere I went further in the matter I had in mind.

Poor Mrs. Hodge, simple Mrs. Hodge. What a cruel fate had left its stain and its memories with her. Only saved from the mire of moral degradation, from absolute destitution, by her strong common sense. She had made her escape into marriage which, if it was not one of absolutely deep affection, afforded her at once a protection and a home. To her ignorant nature, born and bred among the peasantry of the estate, imbued only with the lowest perceptions of the moral sense, she looked upon her rustic spouse principally as a fine animal who had been the means of giving her two equally fine children, and who was a sober and suitable companion in her quiet home. Like a certain class of dependents, becoming fast extinct, her destinies were bound up in those of the great family whose service, and under whose tenure, she and her progenitors had been born and brought up. They made themselves and their interests one with the noble house they served, and in reality looked

113

to the prosperity of their Lord as a necessary assurance of their own.

Mrs. Hodge was delighted to see me. We had frequently met since my first and memorable visit. The anxiety of the good woman on the subject we had discussed had by no means subsided, but she abstained from any pointed reference thereunto, merely contenting herself with a sign and shrug of her broad shoulders, as if to deplore the fact, and my want of appreciation of her views on the subject. But on this occasion she was particularly communicative.

"Ah, My Lady, those big towns like Liverpool and London! The smoke and the fog and the bad air are not doin' you any good, Your Ladyship. If I may make so bold, Your Ladyship is thinner and paler than when you went away. Nothing like the fresh air here, My Lady. In a week you will be a different person indeed."

"I am not satisfied with myself, Mrs. Hodge."

"I don't wonder at it! Why, how can you be? And it's not your own fault either. Ah, dear me, what one has to put up with. Now my Jock—why Lor' bless you, My Lady, there's no holding of him when he's on!"

She had sunk her voice to a whisper. She shut the door of the lodge. She came back and placed herself on her knees before me. It was her favorite attitude. There was something comically irresistible in the semipleading attitude she assumed. I laughed softly.

"Why, Mrs. Hodge, your Jock must be a terrible fellow from your description. I should not care to be in your place."

114

"Wouldn't you, My Lady? Sometimes I think you would, though. He's not much to look at; only an honest plain-spoken lad, but he's true as steel and—and he can hold his tongue. He's as silent as the night. That's what he is! Don't tell me Your Ladyship is content. I've told you already what I think. It ain't in nature—a beautiful sweet creature like Your Ladyship and wedded to . . . to . . ."

"Oh, Mrs. Hodge! What's done cannot be undone, you know!"

"No, but it can be mended. Do you think I'd waste all my young days if I was in *your* place? Not I!"

"What would you do, Mrs. Hodge?"

"What would I do? Well, if I found my husband was no husband to me, but had deceived me into thinking him a *man*, I'd get one in his place. That's what I'd do! So should you, My Ladyship."

She came up close to me in her excitement. Her volubility seemed to carry her away. She laid her hands caressingly upon my knees. She brought her face closer. She felt more confidential—she grew bolder as she saw me smile. I laid my hand softly on hers. She was about to speak again. I motioned her to remain silent.

"I will not disguise myself from you. I do not attempt to deny my great disappointment. That which you related to me on the occasion of my first coming here, Mrs. Hodge, has made a great impression on me. I am young. As you say, I am in perfect health. You are a woman and you know what a woman's nature

115

is. There should be no reason on my part why I am childless."

"No, I am sure of it, My Lady. I know the cause. It is no fault of yours—why should you continue so? I should not be content in your position."

My blood rose to my face, my eyes flashed, I half-rose. The good woman recoiled, half-afraid. I was in ernest now.

"I will not be childless if it depends upon me to prevent it!"

I clenched my hands and stamped my foot imperiously; my breath came short and angrily. Mrs. Hodge clasped her hands together as she knelt.

"Oh, bless Your Ladyship for that! Now you speak like the great lady that you are. Keep to that. Oh, keep to that, My Lady, and . . . try my Jock!"

CHAPTER 6

The night came and also My Lord. After a long drive across the country, we had dined, or rather supped, at half-past nine. The champagne had done its work and my husband was sufficiently lively. As for myself, I was too careful of the part I had to play to allow myself any liberty with the exhilerating beverage. I pass by all details of that unpalatable nuptial couch. Suffice it to say that my wiles succeeded in giving my husband a complete enjoyment of his marital privileges, while my precautions rendered it perfectly impossible for any consequences such as he hoped for. The Earl left my bed charmed with my warmth and vivacity. He was actually proud of himself and his virility.

I cannot say I shared his sentiments. His weak and languid attempts had only succeeded by my assistance, but they were sufficient to convince him of his prowess in the lists of love. The night passed for me almost without sleep. I was restless, excited and uneasy.

The following morning we had arranged a dinner party. It was a hunting reunion. Only gentlemen were invited. I retired early, left the men enjoying themselves over their wine and cigars. I had been the only lady present. No doubt my absence was the signal for the real revelry to commence. I retired to my chamber, pleading fatigue to my maid, and having dismissed her, locked myself in for the night.

My bedroom was on the ground floor. Three long windows opened upon a wide veranda. One had only to step out to enjoy the scent of the roses and jasmine. My object in doing so on this occasion was different. Just as the clock struck nine I stood outside on the tesselated pavement. Someone was crouching in the shadow of the wall. A whispered word, a cautious footfall on the lawn, and I was beside Mrs. Hodge. I wrapped my long cloak around me closely. I drew the hood over my head and silently followed her across the dark lawn through the shrubbery and along the path under the double row of elms which bordered the avenue. Not a soul stirred there after dark, save only coming or departing guests. We kept together in the deep shade of the spreading foliage. We reached the lodge in silence. I followed my conductress through the portal. She shut and barred the gate and door.

A dim light was shed by a small lamp upon the table. Mrs. Hodge took me by the hand. She led me forward. We passed into the room on the right. I stood beside the bed. All had been arranged. I slipped off my cloak and my skirts. I stood in my light chemise.

I had anticipated the adventure with eagerness. Every detail had been planned with scrupulous precision. My feelings were intensely excited. A restless longing for the embrace of a strong man had troubled my thoughts all day. I had been aroused by the faint efforts to which I had submitted on the previous night. I determined to surrender myself without reserve, at least on this occasion.

The stake was immense, the game was well worth playing. No gambler ever felt more enthusiasm as he staked his pile upon a single chance. I had brought all my wits to bear. There is an enormous power for good or bad in a strong will and I devoted mine with all my naturally strong energy to this object. The second title had long lain dormant. There were three sisters, all secretly plotting, jealous of me from the beginning. The dissolute cousin, to whom the usurers were becoming more accommodating as time rolled on, brought no news to lessen his pretensions to the succession. Lastly, and by no means least, there was my natural womanly pride, the instinct of maternity unsatisfied, and the galling feeling that I would be eventually supplanted in the enjoyment of the property for which I had risked so much.

Mrs. Hodge put her fingers to her lips. She held the bedclothes open. I slipped backwards into the feather bed. Two strong arms entwined themselves around my slender waist. They drew me down into contact with a man's

119

hirsute body. I felt alarmed in spite of my resolution.

"Oh, Mrs. Hodge! Pray do not leave me—oh, pray!"

"Hush . . . hush! Be silent . . . he's a lamb compared to what he is sometimes."

I noticed the change in her intonation—the respectful distance, the conventional mode of address were gone. This also was a part of the comedy.

A rush of hot desire passed through my nervous system as I felt the warmth and solidity of the man who held me. That it was a *man*, there was not the slightest doubt. My back, my buttocks, rested against his belly and thighs. Already his parts protruded viciously. His instrument began to insert itself between my thighs. I interposed my hand.

Mrs. Hodge was still beside the bed. I could just see her outline in the darkened room. She held my left hand. My right encountered a monstrous limb. My hand mechanically closed upon this object. It responded to my exciting caress. I felt a bush of curly hair and a muscular pair of thighs. I remained thus for a few minutes. Not a sound was heard. Then the right arm which had held me was softly removed. A large hand inspected my charms. My bosom, my belly, my mount, and lastly the central spot of a man's desires. If my assailant's passion had been already aroused, my own responded to it. A sudden movement served to turn me on my back. At the same movement Mrs. Hodge assisted by a rapid jerk of my left arm. I raised myself in a half-real, half-feigned effort of modesty. Immediately my bedfellow was upon me. In dragging me towards him my nightdress had been turned up. My body lay naked to his attack. He was not slow to take advantage of the position. The fortress lay open. He had to march through the portals.

"Oh, Mrs. Hodge! I . . . do not let him . . . oh, pray . . . oh!"

There was no response from the good woman who had not released my hand. Instantly I was helplessly extended beneath the weight of a man's naked body.

Under such circumstances a woman never complains of the inconvenient pressure. It is true that the elbows of the operator take on themselves a certain part of the load. For all that the position appears to be a normal one. It is certainly the best—the one particularly adapted for the exchange of enjoyment, for those emotions which accompany the act of copulation; those tender emanations of passions stimulated and excited to an almost insupportable pitch; those outbursts of intense ecstasy which are wrung from the yielding female form vibrating beneath the efforts of a vigorous male.

I had seen Jock on several occasions when visiting the lodge. Usually he made himself scarce by slipping shyly away by the back door. I had rarely, however, exchanged more that a simple salutation with him. He struck me as a particularly fine young man whose face displayed more intellectuality than fell to the lot of the rustics around. His wife took pleasure in repeating her commendation of his intelligence, his industry, and his constant en-

121

deavors to instruct himself in the principles and practice of agriculture.

He thus became an object of interest to me, especially after the extraordinary invitation the simple woman had extended to me. In short, I had made my observations. I had matured my decision.

If ever I was in a favorable condition after a forced abstinence to fulfill the requirements of perfected copulation, to relish the joys and participate in the animal pleasure of the act, it was now. My feelings were worked to a frenzy. I remember little of the scene that followed. I received the huge organ of virile manhood with gasping sighs and little cries of mingled pain and pleasure. My assailant lost no time. His arms were around my light body; his own was in determined conjunction with my own. He seemed anxious to incorporate himself with me. He worked with vigor. He did not spare me. He seemed incapable of controlling his emotions.

Mrs. Hodge remained beside me. A few whispered words of encouragement came from her parted lips as the significant sounds and movements progressed beneath her. Then there came a time when I held my breath, when the long pent up forces of nature seemed about to give away. Suddenly I knew the climax had been reached, the end attained. I received a copious outpouring of the prolific balm. Then my companion lay still as death, save for the fluttering of his breath upon my cheek.

I discreetly draw the veil over the remainder of that night's pleasure. It was already late when, guided by my conductress, I again found myself within the precincts of my own chamber. I awoke in the broad sunlight to a new sensation, to a new hope.

* * *

"My sweet Eveline is looking all the better for her stay in the delicious air of Cumberland. I quite envy you that lovely little paradise you have there."

"Indeed, Papa, I feel much stronger. It is the air, as you say, which has done me so much good. I have, I am sure, derived much benefit from my visit there. Endover has gone to his moors again."

"You have not forgotten your promise, my dear child? We were to repeat our experiences of the peephole. Will you join me there this afternoon? I have arranged something for your gratification."

"Do tell me what the nature of it is, dear Papa!"

"Well, it is rather a peculiar affair in which the actors will have no knowledge of the presence of witnesses whatsoever."

"And we are to be the witnesses?"

"Yes, my dear, there are two convenient apertures through which we can enjoy together the interview which will take place. I have reason to believe it will be of exceptional interest to us."

"You quite raise my curiosity, dear Papa."

"I must first say that it is no ordinary thing at all. It appears that a certain gentleman, whose name and personality are both unknown to me, takes a young girl to this place. I am

123

told by my informant who conducts this very private establishment that she is very young, in fact, a mere child, although a very charming and beautiful one. It appears that the gentleman is suspected of a close connection with this pretty child. We shall probably know by and by. Anyhow, it is not the business of my informant to trouble himself about such matters. She is discretion itself."

He well knew my perversion. My passion was all in accord with his own. It was evidently his desire to play upon it, to afford another practical example of the amiable weakness so lightly recorded by Voltaire in the case of the great Charlemagne.

"Do you mean to say, dear Papa, that the gentleman is a near relation? That it is—in fact—a case of incest?"

"I believe it is. Yes, we must certainly see that."

"You charming, darling Papa! How our views agree! How closely our tastes and passions coincide. Yes, we must certainly see that."

"Listen, my child, while I tell you more of this subject which engrosses us. The crime, if crime it be, is as old as humanity. At least as old as the Biblical account of it. Did not the children of Adam and Eve, brother and sister, copulate and procreate? The Bible is full of instances of this original and entrancing weakness. Not to quote the example of Lot, the brother-in-law of Abraham, whose two young daughters, for want of male, as the version goes, but in reality from strong lasciviousness, played with the paternal sugar-stick and made their father jolly with fermented juice of the grape. Then they excited him to such an extent that the vigorous parent laid them both, and all three united in an orgy of lust."

CHAPTER 7

That same afternoon, Papa and I duly ensconced ourselves in the snug little closet on the left of the narrow passage which led to the chamber I already knew.

We had not long to wait. Our door was bolted and the apertures uncorked. We had found that each commanded a more complete view of the bedroom. Our heads were not six inches apart. We had chairs on which to sit, with soft cushions on them. I noticed that the legs of these chairs were covered with India-rubber pads, so that no sound would be audible if they were moved. They were like the caps for sticks on crutches. A soft carpet covered the floor and a padded rest was fixed above each peephole on which to rest the forehead.

Everything was luxuriously complete. Presently I heard the sound of footsteps in the corridor. The door of the bedroom opened. A voice in gentle accents murmured:

"This way please."

The door was closed again after the ingress of the two individuals. Then there was silence, except for the gentle breathing of Papa behind me.

The first who came under my view was a short thick-set man of some five and 40 years. His hair was already turning gray; his closely cut beard and heavy moustache were the same grizzly shade. His features struck me as being ordinary without vulgarity, and he possessed a look of ardent sensuality which, to my practiced eye, there was no possibility of mistaking.

The second comer interested me more. She was a young girl, a mere child, whose age could not have exceeded 13 or 14 years. Indeed, from the youthful face and unformed bust, she might have been a year younger. She was far from being either full-grown or fully developed. What struck me most, however, was her extreme beauty. She had a skin like alabaster, white and soft. She was fair and plump for a child of her age. Her features were regular and good and bore a close resemblance to those of her companion. I noticed that she was dressed in the usual childish fashion of her age; she had very short skirts and wore socks, so that her calves were without stockings, showing the naked legs above the tops of her perfectly fitting high and delicate little boots.

Having carefully bolted the door, the man threw himself upon the lounge. The girl set herself with the curiosity of a child to examine and take note of the apartment. He watched her every movement as a cat watches those of a mouse. I thought I already detected a flash of obscene desire in his liquid eyes as he rapidly scrutinized every change of position. Then he threw off his waistcoat, opened his inner coat, deposited his watch and chain on the adjoining table, and removed his tie and collar.

"Do you see her boots?"

"What nice legs she has! What is he going to do, I wonder? She's very small and young."

"Yes, and so pretty too. Do you notice the likeness, dear Papa?"

We could distinctly hear every word they said.

"Come here, Lucy."

The child obeyed with an air of indifference which appeared to me to hide a certain amount of fear. The man put her on his knee.

"When did I do it last?"

"It was last Wednesday—a week ago—the day mother went to Liverpool."

"What did I promise you this time if your temper was good?"

"You said you would give me a new photographic album and a whole pound of chocolate fondants."

"What! All that? Well, I suppose I must be as good as my word. Now then, Lucy, let's see if you are going to be a young woman."

"Oh, I wish I was already a grown-up young woman!"

"It will come in time—you are getting on fast."

While this edifying conversation was progressing the man had let the girl slip from his knee. She stood between his legs. His left arm encircled her tapered waist. His right played with her ankles, her calves, her knees. Then he advanced his eager hand a little further. Suddenly he bent forward and pressed his lips to hers with a fervent embrace which spoke volumes to us witnesses. He sucked her long and ardently at the lips, with the lustful avidity of a satyr.

"Who told you about kissing, Lucy?"

"That girl at school. She said men knew best how to kiss."

"She was right, my dear child. What else did she say?"

"Oh, I don't know, but she said men like to feel girls about . . . well, you know . . . under their clothes."

"Yes, I think she was right, dear girl. So they do!"

Suiting the action to the words he slipped his hand further up between her thighs. His eyes glowed.

"Oh, there it is! What a nice little slit it is!"

"Oh Father, don't! That hurts!"

We looked at one another for a moment. The secret was out.

"Give me your hand, Lucy. What did you say you might call it?"

"I remember—you said it was a prick."

The man had loosened his clothes.

"What did the girl at school call it?"

129

"She said some other name. I think she said it was a 'diddle.' It was then she pointed to the statue of Mercury on the staircase. But it was not at all like yours. It was very small and hung down. Yours is always upright, Father, and so big!"

He threw aside his shirt. He exposed his naked member with the child's little hand in contact.

"Isn't that nice, Lucy? Oh, so nice? We are all right and quite alone here. You have only to be quiet and play with my prick."

"Yes, I know. Now Mother's at Liverpool we'll not be found out. Oh, my! If I was! How she would beat me! But . . . you won't forget the album will you Father? I'm promised several photos to put in it already."

"No, my darling, certainly not. But come take off your clothes. I want to see you naked. I want to see all your pretty things."

"Oh, Father, must I take them all off?"

As the pretty child stripped I feasted my eyes on the very lascivious exhibition. She was as fair as one of Watteau's beauties and far more comely. A lovely little Venus, with limbs like the most delicate ivory. The man sat at his ease, contemplating the process of disentanglement from the manifold tapes and laces which hindered the operation. His member was exposed in its erected state beneath our full gaze. He had evidently no shame but on the contrary showed rather a Satanic delight in all the indecency he perpetrated.

"Ah, that's right. Now come here, Lucy. What a delicious little slit! Let me feel it. How soft and warm it is! How my finger slips in between the pretty lips! You must never let the boys touch it. You must always keep it for me."

"Mother says that someday I will have hair on it."

"Yes, I dare say. Unless you let me take care of it for you."

The child went down on her knees. She clasped the man's member, a large and long one, with both hands and imprinted a fervent kiss on the livid gland. He pushed forward towards her.

"Now, suck it a little, Lucy. Think of the chocolate."

The young girl opened her lips. The man pushed forward. The big head entered Lucy's mouth. She sucked to order.

"Oh, that is nice! That's delicious . . . stop now! I must suck your little slit. Put your feet on the sofa. Bend over my head . . . so!"

The satyr held the delicate child close to him. He parted the rosy lips of her peachlike slit with his fingers, then he applied his eager face, covering her belly and mound with humid kisses.

"Oh, how stiff you are, dear Papa! This erotic scene is too much for you. Pray keep calm."

The child was on the bed. The man was kneeling over her naked form.

"You won't hurt me again like the last time, will you, Papa?"

"Of course not, Lucy. Only hold still, put your pretty legs apart. Now raise your knees up so. I must lie down on your soft little belly and feel how warm it is."

131

"Oh, but you are pushing it into me. It's . . . it's . . . oh, my! It's too big! It hurts!"

"Be quiet, I say, you young she-devil. You were not making all that noise when I caught you with young Symes."

"Oh, no, but his thing was not as near so big as yours, and he was very gentle."

"Well, if he could have you, so can I. Lie still, I say! It's going in now . . . there! It's half in already. How tight you are, Lucy . . . you young harlot. I'll tell your mother if you cry out. Lie still, I tell you! There, there, now you've got it."

The man began to move up and down. Lucy took a big mouthful of the bedclothes and half shut her pretty eyes.

"Oh, Father, you hurt!"

"Nonsense, Lucy, you must have it all. I'm too stiff to stop now. Hold up! Let me put my hands around your bottom."

The child groaned. The lascivious satyr commenced to move up and down with a regular cadence. It was easy to see that he was in absolute possession. From our hiding place we could see his weapon moving in and out between the girl's plump thighs. I began senselessly working Papa's limb in my warm hand as we looked on. The man stopped occassionally as if to prolong and linger over his pleasure. The girl lay utterly passive, her hands convulsively clutching the sheet as if to fortify her to bear the process of disapportionate coitus with less suffering. Suddenly her father took himself to his libidinous operation with more application. A few rapid strokes—thrusting, straining movement with his little victim, and it was easy to see that his climax was at hand. It came. He fell with a gasping cry upon Lucy's little form and lay bereft of all motion, save for the heavy breathing with which he accompanied the overflow of nature.

"He has done! He has discharged right into her little belly!"

My hand grasped the erected staff—it pushed itself forward. I worked quickly—decisively. A plentiful stream of hot sperm gushed over my tightly fitting gloves. Papa sighed with pleasure and his head reclined on my shoulder. He had succumbed to the pleasure of the scene.

The voices of the strange couple in the bedroom at length aroused us both.

"I want to know what else that girl at the school told you, Lucy. Didn't she say she had two brothers? Now don't hide anything from me, my girl. You know I'll not tell your mother and you had better tell me about it."

"Well, so I will, Father, if you won't be cross. Amy says she has two brothers, both older than she is, and that they taught her all she knows about . . . diddles . . . and things."

"I suppose they had nice little games between all three."

"Yes, but not at first. It was her younger brother, Fred, who began it, she says. He got her into the woodshed behind the house. They live in the country, you know, and there he pulled up her clothes and made her let him put his finger into her slit. Then he showed her his thing and she found that it got big and stiff when she touched it. After a time the elder brother found them out and wanted to play at it too."

133

"Well, Lucy, and then, I suppose they began in earnest."

"Yes, they did. The elder brother had a much larger doodle than Fred. He was 17. One day he got Amy in a quiet corner of the garden and I do believe he would have pushed it into her pussy but it started to rain and while they were sheltering in the greenhouse the gardener caught them. Amy says she is sure he saw what they were doing. Alexander was the name of her big brother and he ran away, but the gardener stayed. He explained to her why Alex should not push his diddle into her slit. He said she had an egg like all very young girls and that she ought to have that egg broken. Then she would be quite a woman and be able to play with the boys and even with the men. She was very much pleased for having him explain all about it to her. She told him she was very grateful to him, so that when he offered to break the egg for her, she thought it was kind of him. She told me that the gardener locked the door of the greenhouse and put her on some hay in a wheelbarrow. Then he let down his trousers and showed her his diddle . . ."

"You mean his prick, don't you, Lucy?"

"Yes, it must have been his prick—like yours. Well, he let it out for her to look at, she says. Oh, such a whopper! And all red on the top. He took her in his arms and pulled up her clothes. Then he pushed his diddle—I mean his prick—up between her thighs and right into her little slit. Amy says he was not long doing it, but that it hurt dreadfully, she is sure that he broke the egg because she felt the yolk all running down her legs when he had done."

During this very edifying history, Papa and I had found it very difficult to restrain our laughter. We were quite relieved when the tender parent began once more to tumble and caress the child.

Her naive and innocent story had evidently had its effect, for his limb stood wickedly up in front of him as he pulled the girl from the bed. He was especially attracted by the rosy little buttocks. Bending her face downwards on the side of the bed, he pressed himself against her back. We saw his rampant member protruding beneath her soft little belly. Slowly and carefully he conducted his outrageous assault, till at last he contrived to sheath the greater part of the instrument in her vagina. Regardless then of the child's complaints, he pushed in until the spasmodic vibrations told that his climax was attained. Whether he had broken an egg or not, we had no means of ascertaining. Certain it was, however, that poor Lucy's legs were covered with something which might have passed for a very pale yolk.

CHAPTER 8

Lord Endover was always on his moor in the North. I was again at Chitterlings. It is true the fine air had done me good, but my residence had not been productive of unmixed advantages.

On the contrary, I suffered from a nausea for which I could only account in one way. The maids in the laundry, I thought, eyed me as I passed. I even caught two of them exchanging remarks about what evidently concerned myself. The old housekeeper took an unusual interest in my movements, I thought she looked upon me with a more patronizing air than ever. What did it all mean? True, there was an irregularity on my part—a certain period had passed—I knew there was an overlong extension of that interval which marked the inheritance of Mother Eve. I admit I was frightened as doubt became certainty, so that one morning I sat down at my writing table and penned these lines to the Earl:

"You have so often and so pointedly asked for news—news which might very naturally be joyful to us both, and I have so often disappointed you, that I tremble and hesitate on the present occasion lest I may raise hopes only to have the mortifying need to dispel them in a future letter. It will, I know, be a source of keen satisfaction to you, my dear husband, to hear that I have the strongest possible reasons for believing that your wishes are likely to be gratified. That in fact I am in a condition at length to become a mother. So you see, gallant man that you are, you are a dangerous bedfellow. How shall I forgive you for the mischief you have wrought?"

My letter brought a prompt reply. The Earl returned. The local medical man was consulted. It was soon an open secret that the Countess of Endover was likely—after all—to provide her husband with an heir, or at least an heiress. At first the news was only whispered through the house. It spread through the domain. It reached the country town. At last it fell with a crash upon the expectant cousin and the three sisters of the Earl. They fairly groaned with vexation. They fell upon one another. At length they all three turned on the unhappy cousin.

What might have happened, I don't know, but fortunately a paragraph in the *Society Peeps* made the matter no longer a source of private inquiry. The necessity for the exercise of dignity they really did not possess obliged them to show a bold front. They received the sarcastic congratulations of the crowd with calm. If they inwardly raged at the disappointment, they were too well-bred to let it appear.

The only one who could not be persuaded to open her lips to the outside public or to show any particular interest in the coming event was Mrs. Hodge, but she returned the warm pressure of my hand with a satisfied shake of the head, accompanied by an expression of stolid conviction which was irresistibly comic, as she whispered softly:

"I knowed it, I did! Your Ladyship did right to try my Jock!"

*　　*　　*

"Ah, my lady, I am so very glad to see you! You do me too much honor. And your excellent Papa, Lord L——, also! Well! so you have come to hear all the interesting facts— all the truths, I fear—between ourselves. A fair, or unfair proportion of lies also, at Bow Street. You will both stay and take a chop with me when the Court rises—a loin chop, of course! Not a chump chop! Ah, you are both so good—how jolly! So glad to see you! Here, Williams, go off to Mrs. W—— at once and get six best loin chops. What! not eat two! Well, to be sure, but your unexpected visit has given me quite an appetite!"

"Really, Sir Langham, it really refreshes one to see you so sprightly and gay—it does one's heart good!"

"Ah, my dear young lady, you are too kind! Pardon me, Lady Endover. I don't think there is much crime on the list today. Some of the ordinary kind: a wife pounded to death. Then there's a sad case, a young fellow charged with forgery. Then let me see—oh, ah—that won't do for you. It's a nasty case but it won't take two of bigamy. Ah, Lady Endover, if they were long. My clerk tells me the evidence is very strong and I think the culprit will plead guilty. You must not be in Court while that one is in hearing. I'll tell them to put it first on the list. It's a way I have at times to disappoint that objectionable class of fashionables who come down here to listen to just such outrages as this."

Sir Langham Beamer drew Papa aside a little, putting a fat finger into a buttonhole of his coat. Then he whispered hoarsely—so hoarsely that I could hear what he said plainly.

"Case of indecent exposure; fellow has been at it for months. His plan was to stand at the entrance to a yard in a quiet street and then when a chance offered he lugged out his . . . hum . . . you know, and wagged it at any likely woman who passed."

"Did he really! How dreadful!"

"Oh, we have a lot of that kind here. Why only last week I had a really serious case before me and sent it to trial. It was a woman who strapped an unfortunate fellow down and then deliberately amputated his . . . well . . . his, you know—*the whole bag of tricks*! The man died, so there was no difficulty in the case, which went to the Assizes as murder."

"I remember that case. The wretched woman gets 20 years penal servitude."

"The Court is open now and the chief clerk

is hearing the night charges. They will not interest you much. There is a case, Lady Endover, I want to dispose of and then you shall both come and sit with me."

Just then the door of the magistrate's private room was opened. A buzz of voices sounded across the corridor. A police sergeant was whispering to the dear old man and Sir Langham took himself away with a courtly apology for his absence.

A short ten minutes passed. Then we were summoned to take our seats. Just as we passed into the Police Court a man was leaving the dock. A warder held the iron gate open for him to pass down the steps which led to the cells below. He stared vacantly into my face. All power of recognition has passed out of that besotted gaze. As I looked, my mind went back to the timber yard and the man in the cloak. It was undoubtedly he.

"A very bad case. He's one of those fellows who are old stagers at the game. He pleaded guilty and got six months—lucky for him! He'd have had two years more if he'd been sent to the Assizes."

It was the police sergeant. He spoke to Lord L——. While we were still in the throng another voice whispered close to my ear:

"From all the rowdy cousins, scheming hags and wicked spinsters, good Lord deliver us!"

Almost before I could rejoin an "Amen" the voice continued but in a tone utterly different in its respectful intonation from the strong nasal drawl in which this invocation had been whispered:

140

"You have saved that man 18 months of imprisonment."

"How so? What can I have to do with it?"

I turned. It was a tall man in a baker's fustian suit. I knew the voice, the figure. It was Dragoon.

"Just this. The chief clerk advised the solicitor, the solicitor advised his client. He pleaded guilty to save the time of the Court. He enabled the magistrate to convict him instead of sending him for trial. He would certainly have had the two year sentence as a previous offender at the Old Bailey. What brings Your Ladyship here?"

"If you will be at B—— Street today at six o'clock I will tell you. I want you to execute a confidential mission for me—for the benefit of another."

"Your Ladyship honors me too much. Always at your service."

* * *

I must not allow myself to forget that these notes are written for my own perusal and reference. No one else will ever read them except him I have designated as the custodian. They contain no more than rudimentary sketches of my intimacy with many of the actors herein. I care nothing for any critic; indeed no such a one will ever have access to opinion of the public, who know me only as what I am not.

My time came at last. All that wealth can do to minimize the agony of maternity I had in abundance. My child was born during the

141

night. Next morning, Endover was ringing with the news that there was at last a male heir to the Earldom, interests and estates. Little Lord Chucklington (the second title had been lying dormant), lay crowing and kicking in the nurse's lap. How I took him to my bosom, how I flouted all idea of a substitute for his own mother's breast, how he thrived and waxed a big and healthy boy—all these things are matters of history now. The Earl of Endover was enraptured. I was an angel. Little Lord Chucklington was a "cupid" and the experienced nurse nearly drove my husband off his head with joy when she reminded him that his infant lordship was "the very spit of himself."

Everyone followed suit and congratulations poured in. The village was illuminated that night. Bands played, drums banged and trumpets rang out as the revelers dispersed in the small hours, sending the faint echoes of their joy on the wings of the wind to my delighted ears in the distant castle.

Eveline had arrived at the zenith of her ambition, but at what a sacrifice! My figure, that fresh, youthful beauty which drove men mad with desire to revel in it, was gone forever. As time went on, I discovered other changes; a transformation which only dawned on me by slow degrees. What may have been a cause will always remain a mystery. It is a fact, however, that all sexual instinct, all desire, had departed from me forever. Possibly some derangement of the nervous tissue had taken place in parturition. It must remain a matter for speculation and conjecture. I never disclosed the fact to anyone. From that time forward I devoted my life to my beautiful boy.

I have yet a few notes to jot down.

"Dragoon" has always been my true and trusted friend.

Mr. Josiah and Mrs. Hodge have emigrated to Canada. They possess a huge farm on the Western prairies. They are rich in the possession of five sons, the elder of which is the mainstay of his father and mother in their agricultural work. Mr. Hodge is reportedly wealthy and all they touch is said to turn into money. Once a year a letter comes, always in the constrained, illiterate handwriting of bony Mrs. Hodge, dutifully assuring me of their happiness. This is as regularly followed by the advent of certain hams and cheese with which my husband is regaled.

A certain tall and fair-haired young medical practitioner one day received a letter informing him that if he chose to make application for a valuable appointment under the Charity Commissioners he was *more than likely* to obtain it. He did so—and succeeded. A second stroke of good luck fell in his way. Another and more desirable appointment soon followed. His keen and corrective powers of diagnosis were soon known and appreciated. His able treatment of his patients brought him renown.

Dr. Brookstead-Hoare did not live to obtain the baronetcy he coveted. His death left a vacancy in the ranks of those members of his profession who as specialists devote their talents to the treatment of women and children. The opening was immediately taken advantage of by the fair-haired aspirant, Dr. A——. He had found time and worked for his M.D. in London and was informed in a certain mysterious manner that the lease of Dr. Brookstead-Hoare's house could be had by him for the asking at a merely nominal cost. He took the hint, also the lease. The aged Duchess of M—— sent for him one day. On the broad flight of stairs which led from the entrance hall, Dr. A——, as he descended, heard a visitor announced.

"The Countess of Endover. Will your Ladyship pass this way, please?"

A moment later a lady passed him going up. In her hand was that of a little boy, bright as an angel, a great favorite with Her Grace. For a second the lady's glance and that of the physician met. A civil inclination of the head and she had gone. The doctor staggered against the wall. He seized the silken cord of the balustrade—or he would have fallen. That which he divined when he reached his new home in the fashionable West had opened his eyes. He knew now, as he buried his honest, kindly face in the cushioned chair, and allowed full vent to his tears of thankfulness and gratitude, who his benefactress had been, and that the world was not all quite one of lust and selfishness.

THE END